BEING EARNEST

Being Earnest

A WILDE REBOOT

A. J Campbell

Quarantine Players Publishing

To my mother who read to me and to the
daughter I read to.

Contents

Forward

Discovering Wilde Through His Play

From the moment I started reading "The Importance of Being Earnest," I felt transported to a world created by Oscar Wilde. His sharp and playful words echoed through the corridors of late Victorian England. This play is a gem in English literature, not only because it is a theatrical masterpiece but also because it showcases Wilde's brilliant and provocative wit. He boldly mocked the society that both celebrated and ostracized him.

As I delved into each character and twist of the plot, I felt a deeper connection with Wilde's perspectives on the absurdities of societal norms. The play was Wilde's way of critiquing the contradictions of a society confined by its rigid conventions. The themes of love and identity were handled with humor and sharp critique, mirroring Wilde's struggles in his own life.

Every line and character in "The Importance of Being Earnest" seemed to carry a piece of Wilde's soul, reflecting his battles against societal expectations and the hypocrisy of the era. The wit and humor were not just for entertainment; they were Wilde's weapons against the constraints of his time, tools he used to challenge and question the status quo, especially marriage. Wilde expressed his views on the artificiality and superficiality of social structures through his characters, using satire to highlight the often ludicrous nature of societal norms that would eventually keep him and his lover from the marriage and connection he desired.

Wilde's art was his way of resisting societal expectations. In his play, people meet only to find that they have been in a fake marriage for quite some time. No alarm is raised at this preposterous assertion in the play. The play's brilliance lies not only in its humor but also in its ability to provoke thought and challenge societal perceptions. It is a testament to Wilde's genius, his ability to weave comedy with critique, making "The Importance of Being Earnest" not just a play but a commentary on the conventional reasons people fall in love and get married.

Vision of the Adaptation

I seek to extend Wilde's original vision in my modern adaptation, infusing it with a contemporary resonance. My adaptation introduces genderqueer characters, a move that both honors Wilde's struggle with identity and challenges the rigid societal norms of his time. In Wilde's era, he was both a figure of fascination and repulsion, a paradox that speaks volumes about societal attitudes toward identity and self-expression. By bringing in these modern elements, I aim to pay homage to Wilde's legacy, highlighting the fluidity of identity in a way that echoes his own experiences.

My version also weaves in modern political reference points. This is not just a reimagining; it is a conversation between the past and present, drawing parallels that are as poignant as they are humorous. In redefining the characters and their dynamics, I aim to sharpen Wilde's critique of societal pretenses, making it more relevant for today's audience. This new interpretation is not just about changing characters and rethinking how we view identity and societal norms.

Oscar Wilde's life was a rich tapestry of triumph and tragedy, defined by his ceaseless pursuit of love and beauty in a world that often shunned him for his true nature. In "The Importance of Being Earnest," I see more than a play; it reflects Wilde's battles with a hypocritical society. Through my adaptation, I aim to bring these struggles to the forefront, employing Wilde's original narrative to ignite discussions on societal expectations and the constraints they impose on our true selves. This adaptation emphasizes the importance of self-acceptance and the continuous fight against societal norms. By drawing parallels between Wilde's time and our own, I seek to illuminate how far we have come and how much remains the same in our journey toward understanding and embracing our true identities.

Who Was Bosie?

Lord Alfred Bruce Douglas (22 October 1870 – 20 March 1945), also known as Bosie Douglas, was an English poet and journalist and a lover of Oscar Wilde, who was sixteen years his junior. The narrative of Bosie and Wilde's relationship is complex, marked by passionate affection, societal disapproval, and personal conflicts. Douglas's privileged yet troubled upbringing, volatile nature, and challenging relationship with his father played significant roles in his life and Wilde's. The opposition from the Marquess of Queensberry, Bosie's father, and the societal norms of the time significantly impacted their relationship, leading to Wilde's legal and personal downfall.

Despite their intense connection, Douglas and Wilde's relationship was fraught with difficulties, exacerbated by Douglas's extravagant lifestyle and Wilde's subsequent legal troubles. The trials and Wilde's imprisonment were turning points, profoundly affecting both men and leading to their eventual separation.

Influences and Legacy

Oscar Wilde was a man of his time and yet far ahead of it. Many sources influenced his works, including his extensive work with 18th-century French playwrights' salon plays. Wilde studied at Trinity College, Dublin, and then at Magdalen College, Oxford. At Oxford, he excelled in classics, demonstrating a profound interest and proficiency in Greek and Roman literature.

Oscar Wilde was proficient in several languages. In addition to his native English, Wilde had a strong command of French and was familiar with German, Italian, and Ancient Greek. His proficiency in French was notably high; he wrote one of his plays, "Salomé," originally in French. This work, first penned in 1891, has entered the canon of Decadent literature and Decadent art. It is notable for being accompanied by the dark, sexually charged illustrations of Aubrey Beardsley and translated into English by Wilde's lover, Lord Alfred "Bosie" Douglas. "Salomé" is infused with transgressive sexuality from every angle. The writer, artist, content, and the proposed cast of the play are all queer in one sense or another. The piece's exaggerated, stylized language and art and their esotericism align with a more classic "camp" identification.

Moreover, Wilde's personal life and trials, particularly his imprisonment for "gross indecency," highlighted the legal and social persecution of the LGBTQ community in that era. Works like "The Picture of Dorian Gray" and "De Profundis" eloquently address themes of identity, societal norms, and individual freedom, making Wilde a symbol of the fight against societal oppression and for individual expression.

Satire and Social Commentary in Wilde's Work

Wilde's use of satire in his works, particularly in "The Importance of Being Earnest," was more than just a source of humor; it was a profound instrument of social critique. Wilde laid bare the absurdities and hypocrisies permeating Victorian society through his masterful use of irony and wit. He deftly tackled subjects like marriage, social status, and the quest for love, exposing the superficiality and pretentiousness inherent in the societal norms of his time.

The play's lasting charm and relevance can be attributed to its ingenious ability to humorously, yet sharply, slice through the facades of society, unmasking the true essence of human nature and the constructs we live by. Wilde's satire was not just entertainment; it was a mirror held up to society, reflecting its follies and foibles in an amusing and enlightening way.

In my adaptation, I aim to extend and deepen this satirical approach. By focusing on contemporary issues surrounding gender and identity, I hope to use Wilde's method to scrutinize and challenge modern societal norms. Like Wilde used humor to critique the rigid conventions of his era, my adaptation seeks to employ satire to explore and question our current understanding and treatment of gender and identity.

This approach is a tribute to Wilde's genius and an effort to continue the conversation he started more than a century ago. By applying Wilde's satirical lens to the modern context, I aspire to provoke thought, spark debate, and perhaps even foster a deeper understanding of the complexities of identity in today's world. In doing so, my adaptation becomes more than a retelling; it becomes a dialogue between Wilde's time and ours, a testament to the timelessness of his insights and the enduring power of satire as a tool for social commentary.

The Evolution of Gender Roles and Identity

In our contemporary society, the notion of gender has become more fluid, and the acceptance and recognition of genderqueer identities are increasingly part of our everyday discourse. This evolution in understanding is something I wanted to capture and reflect on in my adaptation of "The Importance of Being Earnest."

In reimagining Wilde's characters with genderqueer identities, I aim to stay true to Wilde's legacy of challenging societal norms while engaging in the current conversations about gender identity. This adaptation is not just a reinterpretation of a classic play; it is a dialogue with the present, a way to connect Wilde's insights into identity and society with the ongoing discussions in our modern world.

For me, this adaptation is more than a theatrical production. It is a celebration of the diversity of human experience and a recognition of the continuous evolution in our understanding of identity. By introducing genderqueer characters into Wilde's Victorian world, I am paying homage to his spirit of questioning and challenging the status quo while also making a statement about the fluidity and complexity of identity in today's society.

This approach is my way of acknowledging the strides we have made in understanding gender and identity and contributing to this ever-evolving conversation. It is essential that this adaptation honors Wilde's work and resonates with contemporary audiences, reflecting the diverse and dynamic nature of our current understanding of identity. Through this, I hope to offer a fresh perspective on Wilde's themes, making them more accessible and relevant to today's audience.

The Timeless Nature of Wilde's Themes

Wilde masterfully wove themes into his original play — the pursuit of love, the importance of honesty, and the critique of societal expectations — to have an enduring quality that transcends time. As I delved into these themes, I was struck by their relevance and power, which remain as potent today as they were in the late 19th century. In my adaptation, I aim to underscore these themes' timeless nature while offering a fresh perspective that resonates with contemporary audiences.

What fascinates me most about these themes is how they continue to mirror our current human experiences. Despite the significant societal changes since Wilde's time, the core elements of human experiences and desires — love, honesty, and the impact of societal pressures — remain unchanged. This realization inspired me to highlight how, despite the evolution of societal norms and the progression of time, our fundamental human experiences remain consistent.

My adaptation attempts to bridge the gap between the Victorian era and the modern world, showing that Wilde's struggles and triumphs remain relevant. It is a testament to the universal nature of these themes and Wilde's insight into the human condition. I hope to illuminate how these timeless themes continue to influence and shape our lives by reimagining the play for today's world.

Through this adaptation, I emphasize that although our understanding of concepts like love and identity may evolve, the essential nature of our experiences around these themes remains the same. The pursuit of love, the importance of honesty, and the critique of societal norms are not just historical curiosities; they are living, breathing aspects of our everyday lives. By exploring these themes in a contemporary context, I hope to bring a new depth and relevance to Wilde's work, making it not just a reflection of a bygone era but a vibrant commentary on the human experience that continues to evolve and resonate today.

Reimagining the Play for a Modern Audience

My adaptation of the play is far more than just a retelling of a classic; it is a re-examination of Wilde's themes, reframed through the lens of contemporary society. By doing this, I hope to open the doors for a new generation to engage with Wilde's work, discover its layers, and appreciate its enduring significance. My approach is to bring the essence of Wilde's play into the modern day, not by altering its core but by highlighting its timeless qualities in a context that contemporary audiences can relate to and understand.

In this adaptation, I am acutely aware of the importance of staying true to the spirit of Wilde's work while also making it resonate with current societal issues and sensibilities. I want this play to be a meeting point where the past and present can converse, where Wilde's timeless humor and sharp social commentary can be seen through a modern lens. It is important to me that this version not only entertains but also enlightens, offering insights that are as relevant now as they were in Wilde's time.

Through this adaptation, I am inviting audiences to revisit Wilde's themes — the absurdities of social conventions, the intricacies of human relationships, and the enduring quest for identity — in a way that reflects the complexities of our contemporary world. I hope this fresh perspective will allow new audiences to connect with Wilde's work meaningfully, seeing in it reflections of their lives and societies. In doing so, I believe we can celebrate Wilde's genius afresh, recognizing the play not just as a relic of the past but as a living, breathing piece of literature that continues to inspire and challenge us.

A Tribute to Wilde's Enduring Legacy

At its core, this adaptation is a heartfelt tribute to Oscar Wilde's enduring legacy. In crafting it, I am deeply conscious of Wilde's brilliance as a writer and his remarkable courage as an individual who lived authentically amidst the stringent societal constraints of his time. My decision to introduce genderqueer characters and themes into this classic play is a deliberate effort to honor Wilde's spirit, his relentless questioning, and his bold challenge to the societal norms of his era.

In doing so, I celebrate Wilde's groundbreaking work and our collective progress in understanding and accepting diverse identities. This adaptation is my way of acknowledging the strides we have made regarding inclusivity and empathy since Wilde's time. It reflects my belief that art, especially classic works like "The Importance of Being Earnest," should evolve with society, mirroring its changes and growth.

By weaving contemporary themes of gender and identity into Wilde's narrative, I aim to showcase how relevant and revolutionary his work remains today. This is not just a play; it is a conversation across time between Wilde's era and our own. Through this adaptation, I aspire to remind audiences of the importance of continuous evolution in understanding identity and the need to extend empathy and acceptance to all.

In essence, this adaptation is a testament to the power of Wilde's legacy — a legacy that continues to inspire and provoke thought in new generations. It is a celebration of Wilde's fearless exploration of identity and society and a recognition of his role in shaping how we think about ourselves and others. In paying homage to Wilde, I also echo his call for greater inclusivity, hoping to contribute to the ongoing journey towards a more empathetic and understanding world.

The Artistic Merit of Wilde's Writing

Wilde's writing transcended mere entertainment; it was a profound form of artistic expression that challenged and engaged its audience. His remarkable command of language, the intricacy of his plots, and his adept character development make "The Importance of Being Earnest" a masterpiece of literary art. In undertaking this adaptation, my primary objective is to preserve the artistic integrity of Wilde's original work while presenting it in a context that resonates with today's audience.

I am deeply committed to ensuring that Wilde's genius remains accessible and relevant to a new generation of readers and theatergoers. This involves carefully balancing the need to stay true to the essence of Wilde's writing with the desire to make it speak to the contemporary world. The core of Wilde's appeal lies in his timeless wit and his insightful observations of human nature, elements that I am determined to maintain in this adaptation.

Through this adaptation, I aspire to bridge the gap between past and present, introducing Wilde's masterful storytelling to those who might not have encountered it otherwise. It is a way of paying homage to Wilde's legacy, ensuring that his work continues to inspire, amuse, and provoke thought among audiences navigating the complexities of the 21st century. In essence, this adaptation is my contribution to keeping Wilde's artistic spirit alive and relevant, a tribute to his enduring influence in literature and theater.

I hope you enjoy the play,

A.J. Campbell

About Oscar Wilde

OSCAR FINGAL O'FLAHERTIE WILLS WILDE (1854–1900): A Literary Colossus of the 19th Century

Born in Dublin, Ireland, Oscar Wilde ascended as an enigmatic and pivotal figure in late 19th-century literature. His journey from a Dublin intellectual family to becoming one of the most celebrated writers in London is a tale of exceptional talent intertwined with profound tragedies.

Early Life and Education: A Foundation for Brilliance

Wilde's early life was deeply rooted in a rich intellectual environment, thanks to his parents, who were prominent Anglo-Irish intellectuals. This nurturing atmosphere was instrumental in shaping his literary aspirations. Wilde's linguistic prowess, evident from a young age, made him fluent in French and German. His academic odyssey commenced at Trinity College Dublin, where his exceptional classicist skills first came to light. He further refined these at Magdalen

College, Oxford, delving into the study of Greats – a blend of classical literature, philosophy, and history.

Influence of Aestheticism: Art for Art's Sake

At Oxford, Wilde absorbed the philosophy of aestheticism, primarily influenced by his tutors Walter Pater and John Ruskin. Aestheticism, which posited art for art's sake, deeply resonated with Wilde and significantly molded his later works. This philosophy, advocating the pursuit of beauty in art, detached from moral or political messages, became a cornerstone of his literary voice.

Early Literary Career: Diverse Contributions

Post-Oxford, Wilde's relocation to London marked the beginning of an illustrious literary career. His initial foray included publishing a book of poems that explored nuanced themes of love and beauty. His lectures on the "English Renaissance in Art" in the United States and Canada were notable for their insightful analysis and eloquent delivery. Returning to London, Wilde became a prolific journalist, his writings reflecting his sharp wit and unique perspective on contemporary culture.

A Study of Beauty and Morality

Wilde's only novel, "The Picture of Dorian Gray," is a masterful intertwining of beauty, decadence, and duplicity, offering a critique of Victorian society. In "Salome," written in French, Wilde delved into biblical themes, facing censorship but never curtailing his creative ambition. His society comedies, particularly "The Importance of Being Earnest," are celebrated for their satire and linguistic dexterity, cementing his reputation as a preeminent playwright.

Personal Life and Trials: A Tumultuous Downfall

Wilde's personal life, particularly his relationship with Lord Alfred Douglas, catalyzed a series of events leading to his downfall. His legal battle against the Marquess of Queensberry, Douglas's father, exposed Wilde's homosexual relationships, which were illegal in England at the time. This revelation resulted in Wilde's conviction for gross indecency, marking a tragic turn in his life.

Later Life: Reflection and Exile

Wilde's two-year imprisonment was a period of profound transformation, giving rise to "De Profundis," a poignant reflection of his inner turmoil. Post-release, he spent his final years in France, penning "The Ballad of Reading Gaol," a powerful commentary on the brutality of prison life.

Legacy and Influence: Enduring Literary Genius

Wilde's legacy is a complex tapestry of literary genius, wit, and personal tragedy. His works, especially his plays and "The Picture of Dorian Gray," continue to be celebrated for their artistic brilliance and exploration of aesthetic and moral questions. Over a century later, Wilde's life and works remain subjects of fascination and academic study, a testament to his enduring influence on literature and culture.

Oscar Wilde's demise in Paris on November 30, 1900,

marked the end of a remarkable life. Yet, his legacy endures, a testament to the timeless appeal of his literary creations and the profound impact he had on the cultural and artistic landscape of his time and beyond

Oscar Wilde: A Journey from Duplicity to Authenticity

Bunburying in "The Importance of Being Earnest"

In Oscar Wilde's "The Importance of Being Earnest," the concept of "Bunburying" symbolizes the creation of fictitious personas to escape societal obligations. This reflects the lengths individuals go to evade the confines of societal norms, a veiled commentary on the necessity of hiding one's true self in a repressive society. The play humorously critiques Victorian social conventions, emphasizing the absurdity of rigid societal expectations and the importance of being true to oneself.

Duality in "The Picture of Dorian Gray"

Expanding on these themes, Wilde's "The Picture of Dorian Gray" delves deeper into the concept of a hidden self. The protagonist, Dorian Gray, wishes his portrait to age and bear the marks of his sins while he remains outwardly youthful and pure. The portrait, hidden in the attic, becomes a metaphor for concealed identity and societal shame, paralleling Wilde's own life as a gay man in an intolerant society. This narrative underscores the psychological and moral toll of living inauthentically, as the attic, like the closet in LGBTQ+ discourse, symbolizes the space where one's true nature is concealed.

Authenticity in "De Profundis"

In stark contrast to his earlier works, Wilde's "De Profundis," a letter written during his imprisonment to his lover, Lord Alfred Douglas, marks a departure from themes of duplicity. This deeply personal letter is an introspection of Wilde's life, love, and suffering, reflecting a journey from the artifice of his previous works to a raw and unfiltered expression of his innermost thoughts and feelings. The first part of the letter deals with the consequences of his and Bosie's actions, and the second part evolves into a spiritual contemplation, identifying with the individualism and artistic expression of Jesus Christ.

"De Profundis" serves as Wilde's ultimate act of revealing his true self, moving beyond the metaphors and disguises of his earlier works. It can be seen as a profound "coming out" in terms of personal truth and authenticity, showing Wilde's deep, introspective, and transparent side about his experiences and transformations.

Conclusion

Oscar Wilde navigates the complexities of identity, societal expectation, and personal truth through his work. From the satirical "Bunburying" in "The Importance of Being Earnest" and the metaphorical closet of "The Picture of Dorian Gray" to the heartfelt honesty of "De Profundis," Wilde's journey as a writer mirrors his personal evolution. His transition from using artful metaphor and wit to disguise truths to a candid exposition of his deepest self illustrates a profound shift, revealing the enduring relevance and depth of his understanding of the human condition and the societal pressures that shape our lives.

Being Earnest

The Persons of
the Play

Jane Rehoboth, Esq., called "Jane" (she) in the country and changed to "Earnest" (he) in the city. Abandoned as a baby in at the Food Court at Union Station, Jane/Earnest was adopted by Thomas Cardew. Cecily's is Jane's ward.

Angie Monquiff, (she)a wealthy mathematician lesbian bachelorette who pretends to be "Earnest"(male drag) in the country and has a fictitious invalid friend. Loves Ceily.

Doctor Richard Maker "Dick", Board Certified Plastic Surgeon and leading authority in Gender Reassignment surgery. It is said in some circles that only God makes better penises.

Gayman, Butler, and part-time exotic dancer at a SE Washington club.

Lane, Houseboi, in bondage attire.

LadyBird Ball-Buster, is a formidable Real Housewives of Georgetown who would represent 1% of society, values, and opinions.

Gwendolen Ball, Wealthy pro trump gun hun, loves Jane while she is Earnest.

Cecily Cardew, the Trustee of Jane Rehoboth, who falls in love with Angie, thinks she is "Earnest" She is the perfect model of pussy hat-wearing feminism.

Miss Labia Presbyopia, Governess who is so nearsighted she loses Jane when she mistakenly picks up the wrong bag

The Scenes of the Play

ACT I. Angie Monquiff's apartment at the Watergate.

ACT II. The Garden at the McManse, Middleburg

ACT III. Drawing-Room at the McManse, Middleburg

Act One

SCENE

Morning room in Angie's flat at the Watergate. The room is luxuriously and artistically furnished in the manner of a bondage dungeon but with feathers. The sound of whipping and cries is heard in the adjoining room.

[**Lane** is arranging afternoon tea on the table, and Angie enters after the screams have ceased.]

Angie.

Did you hear what I was doing, Lane?

Lane.

I almost never listen to you.

Angie.

I don't play top often but when I do, I make a show of it. After everyone leaves, I will let you tie me up to the cross again.

Lane.

Only if you beg me.

Angie.

What was that? Oh never mind. And speaking of painful have you got the cucumber sandwiches cut for my Aunt?

Lane.

Yes, right here. Just pop it in your mouth. [He places the silver tray so he is presented his balls to Angie]

Angie.

[Bends over in front of the tray for a blow job gag. Makes a muffled sound, then grabs the sandwich between her teeth then sits down on the sofa) Oh! . . . by the way, Lane, I see from your household app that on Thursday night, when Former Speaker Paul Ryan and Mitch Mcconnell were dining with me, eight bottles of champagne are entered as having been consumed.

Lane.

Yes, not including the one I shoved up your...

Angie.

Oh, that is right! Why is it that my butler has more champagne than I do.

Lane.

Many survivors turn to drink. #WeToo.

Angie.

Good heavens! What would happen if I got married?

Lane.

I would have time to heal. I am sure anyone who married you would celebrate with champagne every night. But if I may be permitted, you should get married. I believe it *is* a very pleasant state, mame. I have had very little experience of it myself up to the present. I have only been married once. That was in consequence of a misunderstanding between myself and a young woman looked like he was close enough to 18.

Angie.

[Languidly.] I am bothered in hearing about your other liaisons Lane.

Lane.

I get bothered thinking of them too.

Angie.

That will do, Lane, thank you for now.

Lane.

Thank you, mistress [**Lane** bends over to get paddled, then goes out.]

Angie.

Lane's shotgun marriage aside, I am not sure marriage is completely in fashion at the moment. Now that everyone can get married it hardly seems like the exclusive club it once was.

[Enter **Lane.**]

Lane.

Mr. Earnest Worthing.

[Enter **Jane dress resembling a guy.**]

[**Lane** backs out dramatically with a flourish.]

Angie.

How are you, my dear Earnest? What brings you up to town?

Jane as Earnest.

Work mostly. I have yet another subpoena to serve. What else should bring one anywhere? Eating as usual, I see, Angie!

Angie.

[Stiffly.] I don't have to worry about my weight. Where have you been since last Thursday?

Jane as Earnest.

[Sitting down on the sofa.] In the country at the Mansion.

Angie.

What on earth do you do there?

Jane as Earnest.

[Pulling off her gloves.] When one is in town one amuses oneself. When one is in the country one amuses tech workers. It is excessively boring.

Angie.

Who are these tech workers?

Jane as Earnest.

[Airily.] Oh, neighbors, neighbors.

Angie.

Got nice neighbors in your part of Reston?

Jane as Earnest.

Perfectly horrid! They all speak in code. They don't have a safe word; they have a safe number. It is almost always Pi. It takes forever to say it out loud. 3.14159265358979323….

Angie.

How immensely you must amuse them! [Goes over and takes a sandwich.] By the way, Middleburg is your county, is it not?

Jane as Earnest.

Reston? Yes, of course. Hello! Why all these cups? Why cucumber sandwiches? I thought that this was your Paleo week. Or was it just fruit? All this is not for you. Who is it for?

Angie.

(coy avoiding gaze) Nobody, really. (lifts gaze and looks side-eyed) Aunt LadyBird and Gwendolen.

Jane as Earnest.

Slamming! I would love to see Gwen again. Our texting has resorted to a series of increasingly erotic fruit and veg emojis.

Angie.

Not the eggplant!

Jane as Earnest.

How dare you! Certainly not the eggplant. But I will admit to a cherry or two.

Angie.

You had better keep your eggplant to yourself.

Jane as Earnest.

(grabs crotch to adjust and quickly drops dildo in side pants) Not a problem, I don't always use the eggplant.

Angie.

You get your eggplant anywhere near Gwen and I will turn it into baba ganoush. (pause) I will serve it with fava beans and a nice White Girl Rose.

(JANE comically adjusts the dildo back into place.) Aunt LadyBird won't quite approve of your being here.

Jane as Earnest.

Why doesn't old ballbuster like me?

Angie.

The way you flirt with Gwendolen is cheap and obvious. It is almost as bad as the way Gwendolen flirts with you.

Jane as Earnest.

Nothing about me is cheap. I am in love with Gwendolen. I have come up to town expressly to propose to her.

Angie.

I thought you had come up for leather weekend?

Jane as Earnest.

That too![flashing a bit of leather cuff hidden under a sleeve]

Angie.

Gwen is a true southern belle, pure, innocent, and always armed. If you are not serious then you should forget it. If I ever get married, I'll try to forget the fact faster than Trump's vows on his wedding night.

Jane as Earnest.

I have no doubt about that, dear Angie. There are many men in Washington whose memories are similarly memory impaired. It is practically its own disability category.

Angie.

Oh! There is no use speculating on that subject. Divorces are made in Heaven—

[**Jane** puts out her hand to take a sandwich. **Angie** at smacks her hand.]

Please don't touch the cucumber sandwiches. They are ordered specially for Aunt LadyBird.

[Takes one and eats it.]

Jane as Earnest.
Well, you have been eating them.

Angie. That is quite a different matter. She is my aunt. [Takes plate from below.] Have some avocado toast. The avocado toast is for Gwendolen.

Jane as Earnest.
[Advancing to the table and helping herself.] And very good avocado toast it is too. I will take the carbs for her.

Angie.
How valiant, I am sure she will appreciate that. But you don't need to stuff it all in your mouth at once, though I am impressed with your lack of gag reflex.

Jane as Earnest.
Why on earth do you say that?

Angie.
In the first place, southern Republican girls never marry liberal men.

Jane as Earnest.
Oh, that is nonsense!

Angie.

It isn't. Successful mixed marriages are rarer than a Muller sighting. It accounts for the extraordinary number of people on Grindr that one sees. Like all of them are single. In the second place, I don't give my consent.

Jane as Earnest.

Your consent!

Angie.

Pull your head out, Earnest, Gwendolen is my first cousin. And before I allow you to marry her, you will have to clear up the whole question of Cecily.

[Rings bell.]

Jane as Earnest.

Cecily! What on earth do you mean? What do you mean, Angie, by Cecily? I don't know any one of the names of Cecily.

[Enter **Lane** in a hood, crossing leather braces. He opens the zipper over his mouth.]

Angie.

Stop sounding like a President. [to Lane] Bring me that phone case Mr. Rehoboth left in the kitchen the last time he dined here.

Lane.

Yes, sir.

Angie.

(insistent) Mistress.

[**Lane** raises his brown knowingly, in slight disbelief. Pauses. Starts to speak but doesn't. **Lane** goes out.]

Jane as Earnest.

Do you mean to say you have had my phone case all this time? I wish to goodness you had let me know.

Angie.

Now that the thing is found, there is no good offering a large reward.

[Enter on all fours **Lane** with the phone case on his back. **Angie** takes it at once. **Lane** stands, zips up his mask then goes out.]

[Opens case and examines it.]

My bad, I look at the inscription inside, I find that the case isn't yours after all.

Jane as Earnest.

Of course, it's mine. [Moving to her.] You have seen me with it a hundred times, and you have no right to read what is written inside. It is a very unladylike thing to read private messages on a phone case.

Angie.

Oh! it is absurd to have a hard and fast rule about what one should read and what one shouldn't. More than half of our culture depends on what one shouldn't read online.

Jane as Earnest.

I am quite aware of this fact, and I don't propose to discuss the darker portions of the internet. That kind of talk should be exclusively left on Twitter. I want my phone case back.

Angie.

Yes, but this isn't YOUR phone case. This phone case is a present from someone by the name of Cecily, and you said you didn't know anyone by that name.

Jane as Earnest.

Well, now that I think about it, I do know Cecily.

Angie.

So you do know that woman?

Jane as Earnest.

Yes. My Aunt, a charming old lady she is, too. Lives in a modest estate in Potomac. (reaches for the phone case) Give it to me, Angie.

Angie.

Soon you will say you knew her, but she was the coffee girl. [Retreating to the back of the sofa.]

But why does she call herself Little Cecily if she is your aunt? [Reading.] 'From little Cecily with love to Aunt Jane.'

Jane as Earnest.

[Moving to sofa and kneeling upon it.Grabbing for the phone while Angie dodges, falling about]

Give it to me! Give it to me! [stops running] This is beginning to look like the Weinstein bungalow at the Beverly Hills Hotel. [

Follows **Angie** around the room.]

Angie. But why does your aunt call you her AUNT JANE? Besides, your name isn't Jane at all; it is Earnest.

Jane as Ernest. It isn't Earnest; (raises the pitch of voice) it's Jane *actually.*

[JANE changes stance to a little more girly]

Angie.

Jane Actually? Is this some cosplay situation?(looks Jane up and down)You have always told me it was Earnest. I have introduced you to everyone as Earnest. You answer to the name of Earnest. You look as if your name is Earnest. You are the most Earnest-looking person I ever saw in my life. It is perfectly absurd your saying that your name isn't Earnest. It's on your cards. Here is one of them. [Taking it from the case.] 'Mr. Earnest Rehoboth, The Watergate.' I'll keep this as proof that your name is Earnest if you ever attempt to deny it to me, Gwendolen, or anyone else. [Puts the card in her pocket.]

Jane as Earnest.

Well, my name is Ernest in town and Jane in the country, and the phone case was given to me in the country.

Angie.

Come, old boy, uh girl, you had much better have the thing out at once.

Jane as Earnest.

My dear Angie, you talk exactly as if you were a hooker. It is very vulgar to talk like a hooker when one isn't a hooker. It produces a false impression.

Angie.

Well, that is exactly what hookers always do until you pay. Now, go on! Tell me the whole thing. I may mention that I have always suspected you of being a confirmed and secret Bunburyist, and I am quite sure of it now.

Jane as Earnest.

Bunburyist? What on earth do you mean by a Bunburyist?

Angie.

I'll reveal the meaning of that incomparable expression as soon as you are kind enough to inform me why you are Earnest in town and Jane in the country.

Jane as Earnest.

Well, produce my phone case first.

Angie.

Here it is.

[Hands phone case.]

Now produce your explanation, and pray make it improbable. [Sits on the sofa.]

Jane as Earnest.

My dear woman, there is nothing improbable about my explanation at all. It's perfectly ordinary. My father, Mr. Thomas Cardew, who adopted me when I was a baby, made me in his will guardian to his granddaughter, Miss Cecily Cardew. She lives in my place in the country. Miss Presbyopia looks after her.

Angie.

Where is that place in the country, by the way?

Jane as Earnest.

That is nothing to you, dear girl. You are not going to be invited . . . I may tell you candidly that the place is not in Reston.

Angie.

I have Bunburyed all over Reston on two separate occasions. Now, go on. Why are you, Earnest, in town and Jane in the country?

Jane as Earnest.

(Slyly) Angie, I don't know whether you will be able to understand my real motives.

Angie.

The truth is rarely pure, simple, and or found in Washington. If truth were a real value, at least two TV networks would be out of business, and the internet would be free of disinformation and Russian trolls leaving only room for pornographers.

Jane as Earnest.

I remember last election, I was bombarded with people shouting at me to vote for this crazy screaming man from new york. Whatever happened to him?

Angie.

Oh he lives near here. . . for now.

Jane as Earnest.

(hands in prayer) (Mutters) Baruch Hashem Muller

Angie.

So you are a cosplayer? (JANE shakes her head no)

An actor? (Jane shakes no)

Doing some kinky role-playing game with the house boi where you take turns being Speaker of the House and attorney general?

[Looks quizzically. Pauses. JANE Shakes no]

(Discovery) Then you must be a Bunburyist!

I knew it all along. I was quite right in saying you were a

Bunburyist. You are one of the most advanced Bunburyists I know. I know very few who change genders.

Jane as Earnest.

Well, it is more complicated than that. Ever since I can remember, I have felt that….

Angie.

(interrupting) You have invented a very useful younger brother called Earnest.

Jane as Earnest.

As usual, you are not listening to me.

Angie.

I have invented an invaluable invalid called Bunbury so that I may be able to get out of tedious events and Whitehouse Christmas parties. For instance, if it weren't for Bunbury's extraordinarily bad health, I wouldn't be able to dine with you at Pearl Dive tonight, for I have been tied up for more than a week.

[Offstage: whipping and moans of pleasure as Angie and Jane pause for a second.]

Jane as Earnest.

I haven't asked you to eat anywhere tonight.

Angie.

One does not usually have to wait for an invitation to eat out. It is usually just a pleasant surprise.

Jane as Earnest.

We should both dine with Aunt LadyBird and Cecily.

Angie.

I haven't the smallest intention of doing anything of the kind. To begin with, I had dinner there on Monday, and once a week is enough to dine with one's relations. In the second place, whenever I stay for dinner, I am seated with either no woman at all or two. In the third place, I know perfectly well whom she will place me next to tonight. She will place me next to KellyAnne Conway, who only wants to argue all day with Chris Cuomo. That is not very pleasant. Besides, now that I know you to be a confirmed Bunburyist, I naturally want to talk to you about Bunburying.

Jane as Earnest.

I'm not a Bunburyist at all. If Gwendolen accepts me, I am going to live full-time as Earnest, indeed, I think I'll kill him in any case. Cecily is a little too much interested in him. I am raising her to, And I strongly advise you to do the same with Mr. Burbury.

Angie.

Bunbury. I would never dump Bunbury if I got married I would rely on him even more. A wife that does not know Bunburry will be destined to accompany her spouse to every sporting event in town and some on the road.

Jane as Earnest.

That is nonsense. If I marry Gwendolen, I certainly won't want to know Bunbury.

Angie.

She might. Still, marriage is a set of compromises the woman marries for love, and a man marries for now. Marriage is best when one leaves the door open for others to come in. Two people in a marriage can get lonely.

Jane as Earnest.

Sententiously.] That, my dear young friend, is the theory that porn has been propounding for the last fifty years.

Angie.

Remind me what the current divorce rate is again. All the straight people banging on about the sanctity of marriage all those years when their own marriages are falling apart. Trump is on his third wife and 73 mistresses. Sanctity of Marriage. Why did we fight so hard for it when it seems like no one wants to be in it.

Jane as Earnest.

For heaven's sake, don't try to be cynical even if you are right.

Angie.

We know that marriage is not what it used to be, [Doorbell: An audio clip of Trump saying, I moved on her like a bitch] Ah! That must be Aunt LadyBird. Now, if you keep her occupied with politics so that you can have an opportunity to propose to Gwendolen, may I dine with you tonight at Hank's Oyster Bar with drinks first at Pitchers?

Jane as Earnest.

I only drink at A League of Her Own, the bartender there is hot.

[Enter **Lane.**]

Lane.

LadyBird Ballbuster and Miss Ball.

[**Angie** goes forward to meet them. Enter **Lady Ballbuster** and **Gwendolen**.]

LadyBird Ball-Buster.

Good afternoon, dear Angie, I hope you are behaving your-self.

[raised eyebrow and disapproval in the manner one might observe one's own poo sample.]

Angie.

I'm feeling very well, Aunt LadyBird.

LadyBird Ball-Buster.

That's not quite the same thing. In fact the two things rarely go together.
[Sees **Jane** and bows to her with icy coldness.]

Angie.

[To **Gwendolen**, who is fanning herself with a MAGA fan]
Are you hot?

Gwendolen.

I am always hot! Am I not, Mr. Worthing?

Jane as Earnest.

My temperature is quite elevated just looking at you, Miss Fairfax.

Gwendolen.

Oh! I hope so. I can feel it too. I hope to see many elevations in the near future...up close. [**Gwendolen** and **Jane** sit down on each other's laps by accidentally on purpose. Giggle, then sit side by side.]

LadyBird Ball-Buster.

I'm sorry if we are a little late, Angie. I was obliged to call on dear Ivanka Trump. I hadn't been there since her poor husband's arrest. I never saw a woman so altered; she looked quite twenty years younger. So young, So young. Her father seems particularly doting on her. And now I'll have a cup of tea and one of those nice cucumber sandwiches you promised me.

Angie.

Certainly, Aunt LadyBird. [Goes over to tea table.]

LadyBird Ball-Buster.

Won't you come and sit here, Gwendolen?

Gwendolen. Thanks, mamma, I'm quite comfortable where I am.

Angie.

[Picking up empty plate in horror.]
Good heavens! Lane! Why are there no cucumber sandwiches? I ordered them specially.

Lane.

[Gravely.] We used up all the cucumbers last night. I could pull some of the cond... (Angie glares)..uh.

Angie.

[dramatic overacting] No cucumbers!

Lane. (quizzically) No, mistress?

Angie.

That will do, Lane, thank you.[Lane bows in reverse for the usual spanking, but Angie waves off because of the company]

Lane.

Thank you, mam.

[Exit LANE Goes out.]

Angie.

I am greatly distressed, Aunt LadyBird, about there being no cucumbers.

LadyBird Ball-Buster.

It really makes no matter, Angie. I had some scrumptious tarts with Sarah Huckabee Sanders, who seems to me to be living entirely for pleasure now that she has left the White House. Fake News drove the color from her hair.

Angie.

I hear her hair has turned quite blonde from relief.

LadyBird Ball-Buster.

It certainly has changed its color. From what cause, I, of course, cannot say. She is so blond she could be the new "friend" on a coach, on Fox and Friends, if she were 20 years younger. [**Angie** crosses and hands tea.] Thank you. I've quite a treat for you tonight, Angie. I am going to send you down with Hope Hicks. She is such a nice woman and so attentive to her bosses.

Angie.

I am afraid, Aunt LadyBird, I shall have to give up the pleasure of dining with you tonight after all.

LadyBird Ball-Buster.

[Frowning.] I hope not, Angie. It would put my table completely out. Your uncle would have to dine elsewhere. Fortunately, he is accustomed to that.

Angie.

It is a great bore and, I need hardly say, a terrible disappointment to me, but the fact is I have just had a text to say that my poor friend Bunbury is very ill again. [Exchanges glances with **Jane**.] They seem to think I should be with him.

LadyBird Ball-Buster.

It is very strange. This Mr. Bunbury seems to suffer from curiously bad health. He must be very rich to pay for so much illness.

Angie.

He has Medicaid Aunt

LadyBird Ball-Buster.

Well, I must say, Angie, that I think it is high time that Mr. Bunbury made up his mind whether he was going to live or to die. I don't see why I should have to pay for indulging his illnesses any longer, Nor do I in any way approve of the modern sympathy with invalids and the poor. I consider it morbid. Illness of any kind is hardly a thing to be encouraged in others, especially those who can't afford it. Health is the primary duty of life. If you have health, then you don't need medical coverage. That is why I encourage all the poor people I meet to keep their health in check so they don't need health insurance. I am always telling that to your poor uncle, but he never seems to take much notice . . . as far as any improvement in his ailment goes. I should be much obliged if you would ask Mr. Bunbury, from me, to be kind enough not to have a relapse on Saturday, for I rely on you to arrange my playlist for me. It is my last reception, and one wants something encouraging polite conversation. I cannot have a repeat of the Hillary Clinton - Jill Stein cocktail party debacle back in '16. I should have known then that bipartisanship would be out of fashion.

Angie.

I'll speak to Bunbury, Aunt LadyBird if he is still conscious, and I think I can promise you he'll be all right by Saturday. Of course, the music is a great difficulty. You see, if one plays good music, people don't listen, and if one plays bad music, people don't talk. But I'll run over the program I've drawn out if you will kindly come into the next room for a moment.

LadyBird Ball-Buster.

Thank you, Angie. It is very thoughtful of you.
[Rising, and following **Angie.**]
I'm sure the program will be delightful, after a few expurgations. No Miley Cyrus or Lady Gaga songs I cannot possibly allow. People always seem to think they are improper and either looks shocked, which is vulgar, or laugh, which is worse. Gwendolen, you will accompany me.

Gwendolen. Certainly, mamma.

[**Lady Ballbuster** and **Angie** go into the music room, **Gwendolen** remains behind.]

Jane as Earnest.
Charming day it has been, Miss Fairfax.

Gwendolen.
Pray, don't talk to me about the weather, Mr. Rehoboth.

Whenever people talk to me about the weather, I always feel quite certain that they mean something else. And that makes me so nervous.

Jane as Earnest.

I do mean something else.

Gwendolen.

I thought so. In fact, I am never wrong.

Jane as Earnest.

And I would like to be allowed to take advantage of Lady Ballbuster's temporary absence . . .

Gwendolen.

I would certainly advise you to do so. Mamma being just where she is not wanted to be.

Jane as Earnest.

[Nervously.] Miss Fairfax, ever since I met you I have admired you more than any girl . . . I have ever met since . . . I met you.

Gwendolen.

Yes, I am quite well aware of the fact. And I often wish that in public, at any rate, you had been more demonstrative. For me, you have always had an irresistible fascination. Even before I met you, I was far from indifferent to you. [**Jane** looks at her in amazement.] As I hope you know, Mr. Worthing, we live in an age of alternative facts. The fact is constantly mentioned on certain cable news channels and has reached the political pundits, I am told, and my truth has always been to love someone of the name of Earnest. There is something in that name that inspires absolute confidence. The moment Angie first mentioned to me that he had a friend called Earnest, I knew I was destined to love you.

Jane as Earnest.

You really love me, Gwendolen?

Gwendolen.

Often Mr. Rehoboth.!

Jane as Earnest.

Darling! You don't know how happy you've made me.

Gwendolen.

My own Earnest!

Jane as Earnest.

But...... you don't really mean to say that you couldn't love me if my name wasn't Earnest?

Gwendolen.

But your name is Earnest.

Jane as Earnest.

Yes, I know it is. But supposing it was something else? Do you mean to say you couldn't love me then?

Gwendolen.

[Glibly.]
I only believe in facts as they appear on Fox News.

Jane as Earnest.
Personally, darling, to speak quite candidly, what if it were slightly more different than just a name. What is I was different under these clothes than you would imagine?

Gwendolen.
I am very anxious to see what is under those clothes.

Jane as Earnest.
Well, really, Gwendolen, I must say that I think there are lots options out there that you might consider.

Gwendolen.
[shrieking]

Jane? Jane, how could you be named Jane, I am not a lesbian. Mother would never approve of dating a woman, I myself may have indulged a time or two in my youth at Camp Gloria for exceptionally pious girls. I am sure I heard you wrong; what you said was John. I have known several Johns in my life, and they all, without exception, were more than usually enthusiastic. Besides, Johnny is a notorious domesticity for John! And I pity any woman who is married to a man called Johnny. She would probably never be allowed to know the entrancing pleasure of a single moment's solitude. The only really safe name is Earnest.

Jane as Earnest.

Gwendolen, I must get have a small procedure that will make a big difference to you.

Gwendolen.

A big difference, Mr. Rehoboth? (looks at crotch, moves in for a feel) How Big?

Jane as Earnest.

Did you have a particular expectation that I might fulfill on our wedding night?

Gwendolen.

Our Wedding Night, Mr. Rehoboth?

Jane as Earnest.

[Astounded.] Well . . . surely. You know that I love you, and you led me to believe, Miss Fairfax, that might swipe right on me.

Gwendolen.

I adore you. But you haven't proposed to me yet. If you want me you have to get on your knees before me, a position I hope you will continue often after we are married.

Jane as Earnest.

Well, Gwendolen

[Jane opens her phone and types furiously.]

Gwendolen.

[Gwendolen replies on the phone, this goes on back and forth, resulting in smiles and a thumbs-up acceptance.]

Jane as Earnest.

Gwendolen, will you marry me?

[Goes on her knees]

Gwendolen.

Of course, I will, darling. How long have you been about it? I am afraid you have had very little experience in how to propose. [Jane pops her head under Gwendolen's skirts in such an angle that it appears that cunnilingus is being performed under her ample skirts.]

Jane as Earnest.

[pokes head out from skirts]

I promise I will practice more before we are married. Gwynnie, I have never loved anyone this year more than I love you.

Gwendolen.

Are you sure, darling? I know sometimes men say things they don't mean. I know my old Uncle Steve does. You know the one that worked at the delightful online publication that sends out all those stories about dreadful deep-state conspiracies? All my girlfriends read it. What wonderfully blue eyes you have, Earnest! They are quite, like the blue in the Russian flag. I hope you will always look at me just like that, you look almost like Mike Pence, especially when other people are present.

[Enter **LadyBird Ball-Buster.**]

LadyBird Ball-Buster.

Mr. Rehoboth! Please, sir, you will remove yourself from under my darling daughter's skirt. It is most inconvenient. I did not have her homeschooled on anything but bible verses and veggies tales to have her corrupted by just anyone. I did have aspirations for her to be the President's fourth wife, but that was not meant to be. Sadly, She was already too old.

Gwendolen. Mamma!

[She tries to rise; she restrains him.]

I must beg you to retire. This is no place for you. Besides, Mr. Rehoboth has not quite finished yet.

LadyBird Ball-Buster.

Finished what, may I ask?

Gwendolen.

I am engaged to Mr. Rehoboth, mamma.

[They rise together.]

LadyBird Ball-Buster.

Pardon me; you are not engaged to anyone. When you do become engaged, it will be for the right reason. It is hardly a matter that she could be allowed to arrange for herself like a hair appointment. . . And now I have a few questions for you, Mr. Rehoboth. While I am making these inquiries, you, Gwendolen, will wait for me below in the Uber.

Gwendolen.

[Reproachfully.] Mamma!

LadyBird Ball-Buster.

In the Uber, Gwendolen!

[**Gwendolen** goes to the door. She and **Jane** blow kisses to each other behind **Lady Ballbuster's** back. **Lady Ballbuster** looks vaguely about as if she could not understand what the noise was. Finally turns round.]

Gwendolen, the uber!

Gwendolen.

Yes, mamma.
[Goes out, looking back at **Jane**.]

LadyBird Ball-Buster.

[Sitting down.] You can take a seat, Mr. Rehoboth.

[Looks in her pocket for tablet and stylus.]

Jane as Earnest.

Thank you, Lady Ballbuster, I prefer standing; I appear slimmer this way.

LadyBird Ball-Buster.

[tablet and stylus in hand, flips cover revealing a make America Great Again sticker.]
I feel bound to tell you that you are not down on my list of eligible young men, although I have the same list as the Marla Maples has. We work together, in fact. However, I am quite

ready to enter your name, should your answers be what a really affectionate mother requires. Do you tweet?

Jane as Earnest.

Well, yes, I must admit I tweet.

LadyBird Ball-Buster.

I am glad to hear it. A man should always have an occupation of some kind. There are far too many idle men in DC as it is. How old are you?

Jane as Earnest.

I have often told people I am twenty-nine.

LadyBird Ball-Buster.

A very good age to be married. I have always believed that a man wants to get married because he wants children. Do you want children, Mr. Rehoboth?

Jane as Earnest.

[After some hesitation.]
I do. I have often wanted to adopt a child from China.

LadyBird Ball-Buster.

No grandchild of mine will be air delivered from overseas. I am afraid that I must insist on at least 5 American children before you import any. How else will we make America Great Again?

Jane as Earnest.

What if that is not possible?

LadyBird Ball-Buster.

I know that Gwendolyn will easily conceive again, but if that is the case we make arrangements with some unfortunate women who have waited more than six weeks under the Justice Kavanaugh rule. With so many women pregnant these days, when they don't want to be you would have your pick.

Jane as Earnest.

Did you say again?

LadyBird Ball-Buster.

Did I say again? I am sure that I did not. If you are going to be married you must learn to hear properly. Many a marriage has been ruined by a man who listens too closely to his wife. Now Mr. Rehoboth, where did you receive your education?

Jane as Earnest.

Sweet Briar College

LadyBird Ball-Buster.

Isn't that a women's college?

Jane as Earnest.

It is.

LadyBird Ball-Buster.

Well, whatever antics you got up to on spring break, you did on spring break is no concern of mine. I for one am against extensive education for women, it tampers with natural ignorance. Fortunately, in this government, at any rate, education produces no effect whatsoever. If it did, it would prove a serious danger to the political classes and probably lead to acts of protests. What is your income?

Jane as Earnest.

Between 700,000 and 800,000 a year.

LadyBird Ball-Buster.

[Makes a note in her book.]
In land or in investments?

Jane as Earnest.

In internet startups, mostly.

LadyBird Ball-Buster.

That is satisfactory.

Jane as Earnest.

I have a country house with some land attached to it, about fifteen acres, I believe.

LadyBird Ball-Buster.

A country house! How many bedrooms? Well, that point can be cleared up afterward. You have a townhouse, I hope? A girl with tastes like Gwendolen could hardly be expected to reside in the country.

Jane as Earnest.

I own a penthouse here at Watergate, but it is rented by the year to Madame Fellatio. Of course, I can get it back at six months' notice whenever I like.

LadyBird Ball-Buster.

Pardon me. I must have misheard you. What does she do?

Jane as Earnest.

She is a great patron of young women. She is particularly known in certain circles. They say she if very high up the elephant's trunk. Several beautiful young ladies from Russia stay with her and help her in her religious work. Oh she if very religious. She says she spends more time on her knees than anyone in Washington except Steven Miller.

LadyBird Ball-Buster.

Ah, nowadays, that is no guarantee of respectability of character. What number in the Watergate?

Jane as Earnest. 2169.

LadyBird Ball-Buster.

[Shaking her head.] The unfashionable side. I thought there was something. However, that could easily be altered.

Jane as Earnest.

Do you mean the fashion or the side?

LadyBird Ball-Buster.

[Sternly.] Both, if necessary, I presume. What are your politics?

Jane as Earnest.

Well, I am afraid I really have none. I am a Democrat.

LadyBird Ball-Buster.

You DO KNOW we are Republicans. You will need to correct the error in you political registration immediately. I can't have someone in my family who is in favor of tossing out healthcare and decent wages to just anyone. Are your parents living?

Jane as Earnest.

I have lost both my parents.

LadyBird Ball-Buster.

To lose one parent, Mr. Rehoboth, may be regarded as a misfortune; to lose both looks like carelessness. Who was your father? He was evidently a man of some wealth.

Jane as Earnest.

I am afraid I really don't know. The fact is, Mrs. Ballbuster, I said I had lost my parents. It would be nearer the truth to say that my parents seem to have lost me . . . I don't actually know who I am by birth. I was . . . well, I was found.

LadyBird Ball-Buster. Found!

Jane as Earnest.

The late Mr. Thomas Cardew, an old gentleman of a very charitable and kindly disposition, found me and gave me the name of Rehoboth because he had a first-class ticket for Rehoboth in his pocket at the time.

LadyBird Ball-Buster.
Where did the charitable gentleman find you exactly?

Jane as Earnest.
[Gravely.] In a handbag.

LadyBird Ball-Buster.
A Coach handbag?

Jane as Earnest.
[Very seriously.]
Yes, LadyBird Ball-Buster. I was in a Coach handbag—a somewhat large, black leather handbag with handles to it—an ordinary Coach handbag.

LadyBird Ball-Buster.
Never say that a Coach handbag is ordinary again! I should wash your mouth out with soap. In what locality did Mr. Cardew come across this coach handbag?

Jane as Earnest.
In the food court at Union Station. It was given to him in mistake for his own.

LadyBird Ball-Buster.
The food court at Union Station?

Jane as Earnest.

Yes. Between the Johnny Rockets and the Panda Express.

LadyBird Ball-Buster.

The food establishment is immaterial. Mr. Rehoboth, I confess I feel somewhat bewildered by what you have just told me.

Jane as Earnest.

May I ask you then what you would advise me to do? I need hardly say I would do anything in the world to ensure Gwendolen's happiness.

LadyBird Ball-Buster.

I would strongly advise you, Mr. Rehoboth, to try and acquire some relations as soon as possible, and to make a definite effort to produce at any rate, one parent of either sex before the congressional session is quite over. Do a 23 and me to get yourself some relatives.

Jane as Earnest.

So there is an app for that, but I can produce the handbag anytime. It is in my dressing room at home. I really think that should satisfy you, LadyBird Ball-Buster.

LadyBird Ball-Buster.

Me, sir! What has it to do with me? You can hardly imagine that I and GayLord Ballbuster would dream of allowing our only daughter—a girl brought up with the utmost care—

to marry into an alliance with anything less than a Louis Vuitton? Good morning, Mr. Rehoboth!

[**Lady Ballbuster** sweeps out in majestic indignation.]

Jane as Earnest.

Good morning! [**Angie**, from the other room, strikes up the Wedding March. Jane looks perfectly furious and goes to the door.] [The music stops, and **Angie** enters cheerily.]

Angie.

I have the evite all set up and ready to go. Mazel Tov! Why are you upset? You don't mean to say Gwendolen refused you? She is always saying no when she means yes.

Jane as Earnest.

Gwendolen is fine. As far as she is concerned, we are engaged. Her mother is perfectly unbearable. Never met such a Republican . . . Well, I met this Russian lady at an embassy event. But I told Bobby all about her.

I beg your pardon, Angie, I suppose I shouldn't talk about your own aunt in that way before you.

Angie.

My dear boy, I love hearing my relations abused. After the election, It was all that I could do not to smash their face into the mash potatoes and cranberry sauce. Relations are simply a tedious pack of people who haven't got the remotest knowledge of how to live, nor the smallest instinct about when to die or recognize a Russian Troll on the internet.

Jane as Earnest.

That was a rough Thanksgiving.

Angie.

Amazingly, we made it to the pumpkin pie without a duel. We almost came to blows in the market over the whole milk or heavy whipping cream is best for mashed potatoes.

Jane as Earnest.

Upon my word, if I thought that, I'd shoot myself . . . [A pause.] You don't think there is any chance of Gwendolen becoming like her mother in about a hundred and fifty years, do you, Angie?

Angie.

If a man thought that a woman would become like her mother, there would be no marriages.

Jane as Earnest.

Is that supposed to be clever?

Angie.

I hope so it is going on Insta now. I should get a thousand likes from that.

Jane as Earnest.

You can't go anywhere on the Internet without meeting clever people. The thing has become an absolute public nuisance. I wish to goodness we had a few fools left, at least on Twitter.

Angie.

Oh we do at least one.

Jane as Earnest.

I should extremely like to meet them. What do they talk about?

Angie.

The fools? Oh! About the witch hunts and Hillary Clinton, of course.

Jane as Earnest.

What fools!

Angie.

Did you tell Gwendolen the truth about your being Earnest in town and Jane in the country?

Jane as Earnest.

[In a very patronizing manner.]

The truth isn't quite the sort of thing one tells in Washington. What extraordinary ideas you have about the way to behave!

Angie.

Truth has not fallen out of fashion but has taken a short vacation.

Jane as Earnest.

One day you will swipe right on the perfect girl or boy no judgments.

Angie.

What about Earnest?

Jane as Earnest.

Oh, before the end of the week, I shall have got rid of him. He died in a bizarre protesting accident when he tried to set a MAGA hat on fire that should satisfy Gwendolyn. And I do want to see her satisfied.

Angie.

You have to be very careful with those Chinese-made Make America Great Hats, the tears of the child slave labor that sews them make them highly flammable.

Jane as Earnest.

Toxic exposure sounds a sufficient way to die.

Angie.

Yes, it will start a whole new conspiracy on NotSoBrightBart.

Jane as Earnest.

Very well, then. My poor brother Earnest to carried off suddenly, in front of the White House, by toxic fumes. That gets rid of him.

Angie.

But I thought you said that . . . Miss Cardew was a little too much interested in your poor brother Earnest? Won't she feel his loss a good deal?

Jane as Earnest.

She is devoted to her protests and avocado toasts; I am sure she will find something else to be upset about shortly.

Angie.

What was her Instagram account again, I would very much like to see her.

Jane as Earnest.

I will take very good care, you never do. She is excessively pretty, and she is only just eighteen.

Angie.

Have you told Gwendolen yet that you have an excessively pretty ward who is only just eighteen?

Jane as Earnest.

They will be calling each other besties before the day is over.

Angie.

Women only do that when they have called each other a lot of other things first. Don't you watch The Real Housewives? Now, my dear boy, if we want to get a good table at Pearl Dive, we must dress. Do you know it is nearly seven?

Jane as Earnest.

[Irritably.] Oh! It always is nearly seven.

Angie.

Well, I'm hungry.

Jane as Earnest.

I never knew you when you weren't . . .

Angie.

What shall we do after dinner? Go to a theatre?

Jane as Earnest.

Oh no! I loathe crass distasteful adaptations of classic plays.

Angie.

Well, let us go to the University Club.

Jane as Earnest.

Oh, no! I hate talking.

Angie.

Well, we might trot round to Camelot at ten.

Jane as Earnest.

Oh, no! I can't bear looking at all that nakedness. I am going to be married soon, I can't go to strip clubs.

Angie.

Well, what shall we do?

Jane as Earnest. Nothing!

Angie.

It is awfully hard work doing nothing, ask the President.

[Enter **Lane**.]

Lane.

Miss Fairfax County

[Enter **Gwendolen**. **Lane** goes out.]

Angie.

Gwendolen!

Gwendolen.

Angie, kindly turn your back. I have something very particular to say to Mr. Rehoboth.

Angie.

I am sure I will have no problem hearing from you over here.

Gwendolen.

Angie, don't be so old-fashioned, it's like you are from the 90's or something. [**Angie** retires to the fireplace.]

Jane as Earnest.

My darling!

Gwendolen.

Earnest, we may never be married, but you must know that no matter what rich old man my mother marries me off too, I will always think of you every Saturday night between 8-8:15 during my marital obligations, as the contract specifies.

Jane as Earnest.
Dear Gwendolen!

Gwendolen. Your town address at in Kalorama I have. What is your address in the country?

Jane as Earnest. Arlington, Virginia. You will know it by all the drones flying around. I have furnished half the place by their droppings drones.

[**Angie**, who has been carefully listening, smiles, picks up the phone, and types in the address.]

Gwendolen.
There is good phone service, I suppose? It may be necessary to do something desperate. That of course, will require serious consideration. I will snap chat with you daily.

Jane as Earnest.
My love. My endless love.

Gwendolen.
How long do you remain in town?

Jane as Earnest.
Till Monday.

Gwendolen.

Good! Angie, you may turn around now.

Angie.

Thanks, I've turned around already.

Gwendolen.

You may also ring the bell.

Jane as Earnest.

You will let me see you to your Uber, darling?

Gwendolen. Certainly.

Jane as Earnest. [To **Lane**, who now enters.] I will see Miss Fairfax out.

Lane. Yes, sir. [**Jane** and **Gwendolen** go off.]

[**Lane** presents several letters on a tray to **Angie**. It is to be surmised that they are bills, as Angie tears them up after looking at the envelopes.]

Angie.

A Pill Cosby, Lane.

Lane.

Yes, Mistress.

Angie.

Tomorrow, Lane, I'm going to Bunburying.

Lane.

Yes, Mistress.

Angie.

I shall probably not be back till Monday. You can put up my dress clothes, my high heels, and all the Bunbury suits . . .

Lane.

Yes, Mistress.

[Handing the drink with the flourish of dropping pills in it.]

Angie.

I hope tomorrow will be a fine day, Lane.

Lane.

It never is, sir.

Angie.

Lane, you're a perfect pessimist.

Lane.

I do my best to give satisfaction, Mistress.

[Enter **Jane**. **Lane** goes off.]

Jane as Earnest.

There's a sensible, intellectual man! The only man I ever cared for in my life. [**Angie** is laughing immoderately.] What on earth are you so amused at?

Angie.

Oh, I'm a little anxious about poor Bunbury, that is all.

Jane as Earnest.

If you don't take care, your friend Bunbury will get you into serious trouble someday.

Angie.

I love trouble. They are the only things that are never serious.

Jane as Earnest.

Oh, that's nonsense, Angie. You never talk anything but nonsense.

Angie.

Nobody ever does.

[**Jane** looks indignantly at him and leaves the room. **Angie** took another sip and passed out, ass up over the sofa arm. Lane approaches from behind.]

ACT DROP

Act Two

SCENE

Garden at the Mansion. Cecily is wearing a pink pussy hat surrounded by protest signs held up on a laundry line by clothes pins to dry. She is wearing a shirt that says #RESIS-TANCE and pants with slogans and buttons. There is a small garden table and two chairs.

[**Miss Presbyopia** discovered seated at the table. **Cecily** is at the back hanging signs.]

Miss Presbyopia.
[Calling.] Cecily, Cecily! Please stop painting those signs and come back to your lessons.

Cecily.
[Holds up a sign that says Patriarchy Must Perish. Women Unite.] But I don't like Programming. I want to defeat the patriarchy and run for Congress as soon I am 25 like my hero Occasio-Cortez, [stands next to drawing of Cortez in the manner of Obama's Hope Picture]

Miss Presbyopia.

You know how anxious Miss Jane gets that you should improve yourself in every way. She laid particular stress on your Computer Programming.

Cecily.

Dear Aunt Jane, when will she ever get serious about important things like the plight of the hummingbird, they are dying out, you know, because of all the pesticides we pump into the environment.

Miss Presbyopia.

[Drawing herself up.] Your Aunt Jane cares deeply about the environment, I am sure. Just the other day, she said that she was looking forward to buying a new electric sports car.

Cecily.

It costs more than 4 poor people's annual salary.

Miss Presbyopia.

Cecily! I am surprised at you. Your Aunt put the solar panels on the roof as you pestered her about, changed all the light bulbs to LEDs, and installed a rainwater catchment system, all to make you happy.

Cecily.

It is not for me it is for mother earth. And Jane has not even installed the composting toilets as I asked for Pagan Winter Solstice.

Miss Presbyopia. She has enough crap from her brother that she has to deal with before she starts dealing with ours.

Cecily.

I wish Aunt Jane would bring Earnest here; I am sure we can start him on a macrobiotic diet with regular high colonic cleansing, meditation, and yoga to rid him of his Moscow-leaning ways. He seems to be always jetting off to some meeting in the Seychelles. [**Cecily** begins to write a post on her phone and take funny face selfies.]

Miss Presbyopia.

[Shaking her head.] I think that once the Kremlin has its hooks into you, there is no going back. I pity the poor soul who finds themselves at the mercy of the Kremlin or, worse, the Saudis [Cecily is taking nonstop selfies behind protest signs and tossing peace hand signs] Cecily, why are you always taking selfies?

Cecily.

I post to enter the wonderful secrets of my life. I would probably forget all about them if I didn't post them.

Miss Presbyopia.

Memory, my dear Cecily, is the social feed we all carry.

Cecily.

Yes, but who would be foolish enough to believe what happens on social media? Fiction is not reserved just for Fox News Miss Presbyopia.

Miss Presbyopia.

I wrote a little in my younger days.

Cecily.

Did you really, Miss Presbyopia? I would love to read it. Where is it posted? On Amazon, presumably, though, why do

you give Jeff Bazos any more money... I don't see it. It's like it doesn't even exist.

Miss Presbyopia.

It was about a beautiful virginal heroine who allows a billionaire to tie her up and beat her for pleasure.

Cecily.

[horrified] That story would never work, feminists everywhere would protest.

Miss Presbyopia.

Yes, I didn't think anyone would believe it. Sadly the manuscript was finished but abandoned. [**Cecily** starts.]

Cecily.

[Smiling.]
Did your cloud backup fail? Do we have to check your settings again? (Miss Presbiopia looks flustered) Oh, wait, I see dear Dr. Richard Maker coming up through the garden.

Miss Presbyopia.

[Rising and advancing.] Dr. Maker! I can't tell you what an absolute pleasure it is to see you. [fanning herself] Oh my did it just get warm out here?

Cecily.

It must be hot flashes.

[Enter **Dr. Richard Maker.**]

Maker.

You look a little flustered this morning; there seems to be a reddening of your cheeks. And please do call me Dick.

Cecily.

Miss Presbyopia has just been complaining of the being hot Dr. Maker. In your medical opinion, does she look hot, Dr. Maker?

Miss Presbyopia.

Cecily!

Cecily.

I think your hotness is undeniable, Miss Presbyopia. I think a good doctor should give you a full examination.

Maker.

Of course, I would be happy to check you out.

[Presbyopia nearly faints, but Maker catches her before falling by grabbing her breasts. She slides down on all fours with Maker behind her doggie style]

Cecily.

Oh, dear! Dr. Maker, you should carry Miss Presbyopia inside at once, lay her down in bed, and put some fluid in her immediately.

Maker.

[performs some medical tests like checking for eyes reflexes, she moans every time he touches her.]
Open your mouth wide. Wider.

[places an old-fashioned thermometer into her mouth]
That's it. Good. Very Good.

[**Miss Presbyopia** is enthusiastic with the thermometer.]
Do you feel you can get up, Miss Presbyopia?

Miss Presbyopia.

I am sure I can get up with a little help, then maybe I can return the favor.

Maker.

Call me Dick.

Miss Presbyopia.

[breathless] Dick!

Maker. Shall I take you inside now?

Miss Presbyopia.

[breathy and thirsty] Yes, take me!

[Presbyopia and Maker run off together into the house]

Cecily.
[Picks up books and throws them back on the table.]
Why do I have to learn about these horrible patriarchy-driven stories, where is the Herstory? When the matriarchy takes over, it will change everything! Good wages so people can support their families, universal preschool, daycare subsidies, and healthcare at no cost. It will be a paradise.

[Enter **GayMan** with a card on a salver.]

Gayman.
A Mr. Earnest has just been driven over from the station. He has brought his luggage with him.

Cecily.
[Takes the card and reads it.] 'Mr. Earnest Worthing, B. 4, The Watergate.' Aunt Jane's brother! Did you tell him Ms. Worthing was in town?

Gayman.
Yes, Miss. He seemed not at all disappointed. I mentioned that you and Miss Presbyopia were in the garden. He said he was anxious to speak to you privately for a moment.

Cecily.
Ask Earnest to come here. I suppose you had better arrange a room for him. Not too far from mine in case he needs anything in the middle of the night.

Gayman.

Yes, Miss. or in case you do.

[**Gayman** goes off.]

Cecily.

I have always wanted to reform a Republican.

[Enter **Angie**, very dapper and debonair. Dress resembling a Guy] He does!

Angie as Earnest. [Raising his hat.]

You are my younger cousin Cecily, I'm sure.

Cecily.

I am told quite often how I looked at least 18.

Angie as Earnest.

But you are 18?

Cecily.

I have often said so.

Angie as Earnest.

[Looks at her in amazement.] Age is no barrier to love, as our president says.

Cecily.

Yes, I remember him saying that after a trip with Jefferey.

Angie as Earnest.

Indeed, he says a great many things but seems to do almost nothing.

[they laugh together, flirting]

Cecily.

Aunt Jane has told me all about your exploits. Did you really hack the Pentagon?

Angie as Earnest.

[bewildered] If Jane says I did, then I must have.

Cecily.

You lead such an exciting life. I have listened to Aunt Jane go on about you for years. Did you really meet with Putin? What was Castro like? Is it true what Bernie says about the literacy program? Too bad that Aunt Jane won't be here till Monday afternoon.

Angie as Earnest.

That is a great disappointment. I have to leave Monday Morning to …[stammers for a response guided by the delight on Cecily's face] to attend a meeting [frown] protest? [half-way smile] Protest the counter-protest of the white nationalist group [smile] who are planning on protesting at the supreme court. [ecstatic, clapping]

Cecily.

How brave of you! I knew that you would change your ways in just a few minutes with me.

Angie as Earnest.

Yes, maybe one day you can come with me...to protest.

Cecily.

I would come with you anywhere. But Jane told me you are joining the crew at the International Space Station and will be gone for quite some time?

Angie as Earnest.

The space station?

Cecily.

She said you would be gone for a long time with the training and everything.

Angie as Earnest.

I'd sooner die.

Cecily.

Well, she said at dinner on Wednesday night that you would send you to the moon. I suppose this was as far as she could get.

Angie as Earnest.

That explains it. This world is good enough for me, cousin Cecily.

Cecily.

And you are good for it.

Angie as Earnest.

I don't think I am so good. In fact, what if I was not what I appeared to be at all, underneath.

Cecily.

I am looking forward to discovering what you have underneath it all. I hope I will be pleasantly surprised. One hopes for a big present under the tree.

Angie as Earnest.

Small presents can be delightful too.

Cecily.

[glances crotch, draws back disappointed] Have you been told that?

Angie as Earnest.

[embarrassed[No. No. You can expect a large delivery. (becomes pale and shaky)

Cecily.

Are you quite well? Maybe you want to eat something? I am very thirsty myself (flirty dries imaginary spit from corners of the mouth)

Angie as Earnest. T
hank you. Might I have one of your signs for my next protest?

Cecily.

Just any sign? [Frowns]

Angie as Earnest.

You choose your favorite.

Cecily.

How about this one? [If you quit now, you still get the library. #46]

Angie as Earnest.

I love it. It's very Pence-ive. Maybe you could come to the next protest with me.

Cecily.

Miss Presbyopia would never allow it.

Angie as Earnest.

Then Miss Presbyopia is a short-sighted old lady.
[**Cecily** rolls up the poster and puts it in Angie's hand.]
You are the prettiest girl I have ever seen.

Cecily.

Miss Presbyopia says that all beauty is fleeting and that I should focus on what is inside.

Angie as Earnest.

I would like to focus on what is inside of you as well.

Cecily.

I am sure you will find time to get to know me [eye raise] in depth.

[They pass into the house. **Miss Presbyopia** and **Dr. Maker** return.]

Miss Presbyopia.

You are too much alone, dear Dr. Maker. You should get married.

Maker.

[With a shudder.] It is isolating being the best plastic surgeon in Washington. People find it harder to talk out of both sides of their mouth when their lips are pulled tight. [demonstrates]

Miss Presbyopia.

[Sententiously.] You are doing the politicians and societies of Washington, DC a great service. But what about you, Doctor, how are you getting serviced?

Maker.

There is a place at the Watergate...

Miss Presbyopia.

[interrupts, realizing the reference] But where is Cecily?

Maker.

Perhaps she is still studying.

[Enter **Jane** slowly from the back of the garden. He is dressed in the deepest mourning, looking very similar to Breakfast at Tiffany's.]

Miss Presbyopia.

This is indeed a surprise.

Jane.

[Shakes **Miss Presbyopia's** hand in a tragic manner.]

I have returned sooner than I expected. Dr. Maker, I hope you are well?

Maker.

Dear Jane, I trust you are coming home from a fabulous party?

Jane.

No I am in morning for my brother.

Miss Presbyopia.

He didn't get caught in Thailand again? Does he need a lawyer?

Maker.

If you can wait, Michael Cohen is about to be available.

Jane.

[Shaking her head.] Dead!

Maker.

Your brother Earnest dead?

Jane.

Quite dead.

Miss Presbyopia.

May his memory be for a lesson.

Maker. The wages of sin are often paid too early. Only Trump's wives have been more forgiving than you.

Jane.

Yes it has been very sad.

Maker.

Very sad indeed. Were you with him at the end?

Jane.

No. He died in Paris.

Maker.

Well at least he was in a city he loved.

Jane.

He died in DC in the Watergate.

Miss Presbyopia.

That is shocking!

Maker.

[inquisitive] Yes, quite shocking. Paris is still the same...never mind DM me later.

Jane.

His only desire is to have his ashes spread at Hanes Point,

where the statue of the Awakening used to be. He said he would often go there late at night.

Maker.

[Shakes his head.] I always thought people went there for encounters of a particular kind.

Miss Presbyopia.

Like to feed the ducks?

Jane.

Ah! That reminds me, you mentioned you do gender re-assignment surgery I think, Dr. Maker? [**Dr. Maker** looks astounded.] Of course, you are considered one of the best, aren't you?

Miss Presbyopia.

I have often wanted to see some of your work up close for some time now.

Maker.

Are you asking for a friend?

Jane.

Um...

Maker.

Jane, some policies must be followed, time that must be taken. My schedule is very full.

Jane.

[(writes a number down on paper] I would be willing to pay a premium.

Maker.

A whole just opened up in my schedule.

Jane.

Wonderful, make sure mine is closed. We should talk about length later.

Maker.

You mean at length.

Jane.
No.

Maker.

You need have no apprehensions. I am a professional.

Jane.

Oh, I might trot round about five with a few samples to give you an idea of what I, I mean, she might want.

Maker.

Perfectly, perfectly!

Jane.

Oh! Would 5:30 five do? Before then, I have the Senate Majority Leader coming in for an evaluation.

Jane.

He wants to become a woman?

Maker.

No, I am fitting him for a set of balls, he lost his in a tragic voting incident in 2016 [Takes out watch.] And now, dear Msss, I will no longer intrude into a house of sorrow.

Miss Presbyopia.

You will get through this.

[Enter **Cecily** from the house.]

Cecily.

Aunt Jane! Did you have Breakfast at Tiffany's again? For the last time, we feminists do not like that story. Holly Go-lightly was abused by the patriarchy and passed around like a handmaiden. No true feminist would ever read that story. It should be banned from all libraries and Amazon immediately.

Miss Presbyopia.

[sheds fake tears at her protege] They grow up so fast.

Maker.

Next she will be demanding that all men get vasectomies so women don't have to take birth control anymore.

[**Cecily** goes towards **Jane**; she kisses her brow in a melancholy manner.]

Cecily.

It would be a good start. [to Jane] I have got such a surprise for you. Who do you think is in the dining room? Your brother!

Jane.
Who?

Cecily.
Your brother Earnest. He arrived about half an hour ago.

Jane.
I have no brother.

Cecily.
No matter what he has done, no matter how many lies he has told, how many Republicans he has voted for, and porn stars he has paid off, he is still your brother. [Runs back into the house.]

Maker.
It is a medical miracle.

Miss Presbyopia.
It's like he has come back from the dead, like a zombie.

Jane.
Unless the man in the dining room is a zombie, someone owes me an explanation.

[Enter **Angie** and **Cecily** hand in hand. They come slowly up to **Jane.**]

Jane.

Good heavens! [Motions **Angie** away.]

Angie as Earnest.

….[confused at Jane's Dress] I have come down from town to tell you that I am very sorry for all the trouble I have given you, and that I intend to lead a better life in the future. [**Jane** glares at him and does not take his hand.]

Cecily.

Aunt Jane, you are not going to refuse your own brother's hand?

Jane.

Nothing will induce me to take his hand. I know where it has been.

Cecily.

Aunt Jane, do be nice. There is some good in every one. Earnest has just been telling me about his poor sick friend Bunbury who needs his constant support and attention. He even started a GoFundMe for his medical bills.

Jane.

Oh! he has been talking about Bunbury, has he?

Cecily.

Yes, he has told me all about poor Mr. Bunbury, and his terrible state of health.

Jane.

Bunbury! Well, I won't have him talk to you about Bunbury or about anything else.

Angie as Earnest.

Of course I admit that the faults were all on my side. But I must say that I think that Sister Jane's coldness to me is peculiarly painful. I expected a more enthusiastic welcome, especially considering it is the first time I have come here.

Cecily.

Aunt Jane, if you don't shake hands with Earnest I will never forgive you.

Jane.

Never forgive me?

Cecily.

Never, never, never!

Jane.

Well, this is the last time I shall ever do it. [Shakes with **Angie** and glares.]

Maker.

It is lovely to see such a perfect reconciliation. Perhaps after this Cecily you can go work some magic on the democratic party.

Miss Presbyopia.

Cecily, Your work here is done.

Cecily.

Certainly, Miss Presbyopia. My Andy Cohen, Real House-wives moment is over.

Maker.

It would have made a great episode.

Miss Presbyopia.

Maybe it would have been better with more table flipping.

Cecily.

Next time... [They all go off except **Jane** and **Angie**.]

Jane.

You bitch, Angie, you must get out of this place as soon as possible. I don't allow any Bunburying here.

[Enter **Gayman**.]

Gayman.

I have put Earnest's things in the room next to yours, sir. I suppose that is all right?

Jane.

What?

Gayman.

Earnest's luggage, mam. I have unpacked it and put it in the room next to your own.

Jane.

His luggage?

Gayman.

Yes, sir. Three rolling suitcases.

Angie as Earnest.

I am afraid I can't stay more than a week this time.

Jane.

Gayman, order an Uber at once. Earnest has been suddenly called back to town.

Gayman.

Yes, mam.

[Goes back into the house.]

Angie as Earnest.

What a fearful liar you are, "Jane". Lovely dress by the way. You look like a drag queen walking home at 4 am. I am staying right here.

Jane.

No, you are not.

Angie as Earnest.

[pulls out phone] I haven't heard anyone call me.

Jane.

Your duty as a woman calls you back.

Angie as Earnest.

Being a woman has never interfered with my pleasures to the smallest degree. It is the manly duties that have always intrigued me.

Jane. I can quite understand that.

Angie as Earnest.

Well, Cecily is a darling.

Jane.

You are not to talk of Cecily like that. I don't like it.

Angie as Earnest.

Well, I don't like your clothes. You look perfectly ridiculous in a little black dress. Why on earth don't you go up and change?

Jane.

You are not staying with me for a whole week as a guest or anything else. You have got to leave.

Angie as Earnest.

But I want to spend more time in the country.

Jane.

Well, will you go if I change my clothes?

Angie as Earnest.

Yes, if you are not too long.

Jane.

I will be as long as I need to be Jane, not a bit less, hopefully, a lot more.

Angie as Earnest.

You look ridiculous in a dress anyway; it's like you are a Fox Money Honey.

Jane.

What about your questionable sartorial choices? You look like the love child of James Bond and Anderson Cooper. This Bunburying, as you call it, has not been a great success for you.

[Goes into the house.]

Angie as Earnest.

I think it has been a great success. I'm in love with Cecily, and that is everything.

[Enter **Cecily** at the back of the garden. She picks up the can and begins to water the flowers.] But I must see her before I go and make arrangements for another Bunbury. Ah, there she is.

Cecily.

Oh, I merely came back to collect my posters. I thought you were with Aunt Jane.

Angie as Earnest.

She's gone to order an Uber for me.

Cecily.

Oh, are you going to a Jeweler? Size 6 and make it con-flict-free.

Angie as Earnest.

[types into phone] Jane is sending me away.

Cecily.

But I don't want you to leave unless you will protest some vile evil in the world. [checks on phone] Is Mike Pence still in town?

Angie as Earnest.

I will try to find a march just for you. You will see the pictures on my Instagram.

Cecily.

I feel like I have known you my whole life; leaving you now after only knowing you briefly would be a trauma I would have to discuss for years in therapy.

Angie as Earnest.

At least I will be in your thoughts.

[Enter **Gayman**.]

Gayman.

The Uber is at the door, sir. [**Angie** looks appealingly at **Cecily**.]

Cecily.

It can wait, Gayman, for . . . five minutes.

Angie as Earnest.

It will be longer than five minutes, I assure you.

Gayman.

Yes, miss [Exit **Gayman**.]

Angie as Earnest.

I hope, Cecily, I won't offend you by saying that although I admire your warrior princess spirit if you forgive the cultural appropriation, I find your outer beauty not displeasing.

Cecily.

I don't experience that as a microaggression. I will quote you in my Instagram story. [begins typing on the phone.]

Angie as Earnest.

You really keep up with your social media. I'd give anything to look at it. What is your handle?

Cecily.

Oh no. [Puts her hand over it.] Even though the whole world can read my innermost thoughts, my deepest longings, and my dreams, you can't till I know you better.

Angie as Earnest.

[Somewhat taken aback.] I hope to know you so well that you will let me change your status one day.

Cecily.

That would be a big step indeed. [Writes as **Angie** speaks.]

Angie as Earnest.

[Speaking very rapidly.] Cecily, since 20 minutes ago, when I first met you, I could not help but think how brilliant you were and how I am hopelessly in love with the very idea of you.

Cecily.

The very idea of me? I am in love with the idea of you too. We could be married [Angie backs away], and you would be An Ideal Husband.

Angie as Earnest.

Cecily!

[Enter **Gayman**.]

Gayman.

The car is waiting, sir.

Angie as Earnest.

Send it away.

Gayman.

[Looks at **Cecily**, who makes no sign.] Yes, sir.

[**Gayman** retires.]

Cecily.

Aunt Jane expected you to be gone, but you are still here.

Angie as Earnest.

I don't care what Jane wants. I want you, Cecily. Will you marry me?

Cecily.

Don't be silly! Of course. Why, we have been engaged for the last three months.

Angie as Earnest.

For the *last three* months?

Cecily.

Yes.

Angie as Earnest. How did I propose?

Cecily.

Ever since I heard about your exploits, how you rammed through Brexit, hacked the voting systems in Florida in 2000 and 2016, I knew you were the one I wanted.

Angie as Earnest.

What was the day?

Cecily.

On the 14th of February. Herteronormative, I know, but even ar radical pro-feminist like me likes a little convention. I could not wait for you to meet me any longer, and I had to propose to myself.

Angie.

It's all very one-sided, Cecily.

Cecily.

I am a modern independent woman; I will not simply wait around for a man to validate me. So I did it for you. I sustained myself through your absence by reading your posts.

Angie as Earnest.

[nervously] My posts? I thought I had deleted all of them. How many of them did you read? [flicks through phone] You didn't read the one about the...with..the...thing with Mitch McConnell?

Cecily.

You don't have to remind me how neglectful you have been, so I had to write the posts for you.

Angie as Earnest.

Maybe I should read them, Cecily?

Cecily.

That would hardly be appropriate. Then you would know what I really feel about you. And that can't happen till at least 6 months of marriage. Besides, I don't want to relive the deep depression that I fell into when I was forced to break off our engagement.

Angie as Earnest.

Why did we break up?

Cecily.

We could not agree if Pence should be indicted first. Or should he step down in a grand act of reconciliation towards our democracy? I even changed my Facebook status. You can see the entry if you like. [Shows phone.] 'I broke off my engagement with Earnest. I feel it is better to do so. He was wrong, and we must remove the people from our lives who do not agree with us. Beautiful Sunset tonight.'

Angie as Earnest.

Why would you cut me out of your life just because we disagree?

Cecily.

I can only be with someone fully if they agree with every-thing I believe in.

Angie as Earnest.

[Crossing to her and kneeling.] I will never disagree with you again.

Cecily.

[She kisses her, she puts her fingers through her hair.] Is your hair natural?

Angie as Earnest.

Some of it.

Cecily.

I am so glad our children will be stunning.

Angie as Earnest.

You'll never break off our engagement again, Cecily?

Cecily.

I wasn't sure at first, but now that I have finally met you, I feel all my uncertainty is ending. But the deciding factor has been and will always be your name.

Angie as Earnest.

Yes, of course. [Nervously.]

Cecily.

I have always wanted to marry someone by the name of Earnest. [Angie rises, Cecily also.] It is such an old-fashioned name, but Being Earnest has fallen quite out of fashion in Washington.

Angie as Earnest.

But, my dear, do you mean to say you could not love me if I had some other name or if I were different under these clothes?

Cecily.

But what name?

Angie as Earnest.

Oh, any name you like—Angie—for instance . . .

Cecily.

But I don't like the name, Angie.

Angie.

I really can't see why you should object to the name of Angie. It is not at all a bad name. It is rather an aristocratic name. But seriously, Cecily . . . [Moving to her] . . . if my name was Angie, couldn't you love me?

Cecily.

[Rising.] Oh! (ridiculously excited) Are you transgender? Angie is a girl's name, after all. I am so thrilled! [shakes no], nonbinary [shakes no], gender nonconforming [shakes no]?

Angie as Earnest.

No, Cecily just a lesbian! A woman who loves women.[Picking up hat.]

Cecily.

Just a lesbian? That is not very common. Surely you are something else too?

Angie.

No just a lesbian.

Cecily.

You should be proud of who you are. I, of course, support all 23 gender expressions. Are you sure?

Angie.

Yes, still just a lesbian.

Cecily.

Oh! [disappointed] of course, do not recognize gender in love, it is so last century. While I appreciate your choice to be a woman, I have already decided that I will be a human entity named Earnest. Are you sure you have not felt like a man trapped in a woman's body your whole life?

Angie as Earnest.

I do think I would know.

Cecily.

I don't know why your generation spent so much time coming out when in fact there never was a closet.

Angie as Earnest.

If there were no closets, Cecily, why are so many people beat up for coming out of them? It seems your generation has found a whole new closet. Speaking of closets, would it be ok if I slipped out of these clothes now?

Cecily. [looks nervous] Someone could walk in.

Angie as Earnest.

I will go to my room and change.

Cecily. "
Considering that we have been engaged since February the 14th, and that I only met you today for the first time, I think it

is rather hard that you should leave me for such a long period of half an hour. Couldn't you make it twenty minutes?

Angie.

I'll be back in no time.

[Kisses her and rushes down the garden.]

Cecily.

What an impetuous girl she is! I like her hair so much. I must post about her proposal immediately. Now I can be a true intersectional feminist.

[Enter **Gayman.**]

Gayman.

Gwendolyn Fairfax has just called to see Earnest. On very important business.

Cecily.

Earnest is upstairs. Isn't Jane in her library?

Gayman.

Jane went over in the direction of the good doctor's consultation room, not that I know where it is for sure, having never needed his services. [Cecily raises her brow and glances at the crotch region.]

Cecily.

Ask the lady to come out here. And you can bring tea.

Gayman.

Yes, Miss. [Goes out.]

Cecily.

Miss Fairfax! I suppose one of the many good elderly women who are associated with Aunt Jane in some of his philanthropic work in DC. I hope she is not one of those that just do it to brag about it on Facebook.

[Enter **Gayman**.]

Gayman.

Miss Gwendolyn.

[Enter **Gwendolen**.]

[Exit **Gayman**.]

Cecily.

[Advancing to meet her.] Let me introduce myself to you. My name is Cecily Cardew. I use the They/Them pronouns.

Gwendolen.

Whose they?

Cecily.

You may use They and Them pronouns to address me. I prefer not to use male or female pronouns at all.

Gwendolen.

I don't understand, Them?

Cecily.

Yes?

Gwendolen.

Them Who?

Cecily. Them Me.

Gwendolen.

Is there someone else inside [looking very closely near Cecily.] there with you? I had an Aunt like this, we locked her in the basement when she started to want to be called by a different name. [loudly] Who am I speaking to now?

Cecily.

Cecily.

Gwendolen.

Well, if anyone else comes out, tell them I say howdy too. Bless your heart.

Cecily.

What pronouns should I use for you?

Gwendolen.

My dear, should that not be obvious I am a woman? Have you been out in the sun too long?

Cecily.

It is considered impolite to assume. What if I guessed wrong?

Gwendolen.

Oh dear, you are worse off than I thought. You go ahead and do your best, precious.

Cecily.

I would not want to offend you by mistaking you for a woman when you are a man. You might need years of therapy to get over an oppressive act like that.

Gwendolen.

You poor thing, you may call me, she, 'cause I am one.

Cecily.

So it is all settled.

Gwendolen.

Perhaps this might be a favorable opportunity for my mentioning who I am. My father is Mr. Ball. You have never heard of papa, I suppose?

Cecily.

I don't think so. It is hard to find any Balls in Washington.

Gwendolen.

Outside the family circle, papa, I am glad to say, is entirely unknown. I think that is quite as it should be. The home seems to me to be the proper sphere for the man. And certainly, once a man begins to neglect his domestic duties, he becomes painfully effeminate, does he not? And I don't like that. It makes men so very attractive. Cecily, mamma, whose views on education are remarkably strict, has made me extremely short-sighted; it is part of her system, so do you mind my looking at you through my augmented reality app?

Cecily.

Oh! not at all, Gwendolen. I am very fond of being looked at.

Gwendolen.

[After examining **Cecily** carefully through a google glass her phone.] You are here on a short visit, I suppose.

Cecily.

Oh no! I live here.

Gwendolen.

[Severely.] Really? Your mother, no doubt, or some female relative of advanced years, resides here also?

Cecily.

Oh no! I have no mother or father.

Gwendolen.

Indeed? There seems to be a lot of that going on.

Cecily.

My dear guardian, with the assistance of Miss Presbyopia, has the arduous task of educating me as best they can, but like most women my age I was raised by social media. I suppose a woman of your generation was raised on television.

Gwendolen.

Television! Not even cable! The light must be faulty out here. Who is Your Guardian?

Cecily.

Yes, I am Jane's ward.

Gwendolen.

Oh! [Relieved] I am very fond of you, Cecily; I have liked you since I met you! Your makeup looks exquisite.

Cecily.

I am not wearing any makeup. I don't believe in it. Fresh natural beauty is better. Makeup is a method of repression. [Gwen is putting on lipstick]

Gwendolen.

[hastily puts away makeup] I barely wear any myself.

Cecily.

It looks like you are wearing an entire Sephora.

Gwendolen.

My own Earnest likes a woman who makes an effort for her man.

Cecily.

Maybe they want a partner who needs less effort. Did you say, Earnest?

Gwendolen.

We are back to they again. Yes, we are recently engaged. **He** has become everything to me. I can't wait till we are married.

Cecily.

I am recently engaged as well to Earnest.

Gwendolen.

[Sitting down again.] What a remarkable coincidence.

Cecily.

Yes, amazing.

Gwendolen.

Earnest is full of surprises.

Cecily.

Yes, I have recently been surprised by them.

Gwendolen.

[Inquiringly.] I beg your pardon.

Cecily.

[Rather shy and confidingly.] Dearest Gwendolen, there is no reason why I should make a secret of it to you. The person you know as Earnest and I are engaged to be married!

Gwendolen.

[Quite politely, rising.] My darling Cecily, I think there must be some slight error. Earnest is engaged to me. You must be mistaken, Earnest for Ernesto; maybe a gardener around here?

Cecily.

[Very politely, rising.] I am afraid you must be under some misconception. Earnest proposed to me exactly ten minutes ago. [Shows phone.]

Gwendolen.

[Examines diary carefully.]

It is very curious, for he asked me to be his lawfully wedded wife yesterday afternoon at 5.30 pm. Here you can see my page.I am so sorry, dear Cecily if it disappoints you, but I am afraid I have the prior claim.

Cecily.

It would distress me more than I can tell you, dear Gwendolen, if it caused you any mental or physical anguish, but I feel bound to point out that since Earnest proposed to you, they have changed their mind.

Gwendolen.

[Meditatively.] Are we back to they again? Dear, you really have got to get out of this sun. Earnest is a man; you are clearly delusional, a result no doubt of exposure to liberal feminism.

Cecily.

[Thoughtfully and sadly.] Whatever mistakes Earnest has made in the past, will be forgiven. Clearly this was the last fling before settling down.

Gwendolen.

A fling! I am hardly a side dish, I am the whole entree.

Cecily.

Maybe Earnest was just tired of having to lift such a heavy plate.

Gwendolen.

[Satirically.] Heavy indeed, I weigh the same as I did when I was crowned Miss Sweet Potato Pie.

[Enter **Gayman**, followed by the footman. He carries a salver, tablecloth, and plate stand. **Cecily** is about to retort. The presence of the servants exercises a restraining influence, under which both girls chafe.]

Gayman.

Careful not to spill the tea, Ms.

Cecily.

[Sternly, in a calm voice.] Yes,

[**Gayman** begins to clear the table and lay the cloth. A long pause. **Cecily** and **Gwendolen** glare at each other.]

Gwendolen.

This is a lovely part of the country. Are there many golf courses around here? I do so like to play a round or two.

Cecily.

I don't doubt that you play around.

Gwendolen.

Do you play tennis? I myself am a champion tennis player.

Cecily.

[Sweetly.] You do seem to be into games.

[**Gwendolen** bites her lip and beats her foot nervously with her parasol.]

Gwendolen.

[Looking round.] This is a lovely garden.

Cecily.

So glad you like it, Gwendolen.

Gwendolen.

So many flowers in the country, they are quite common.

Cecily.

Beautiful flowers are in the country, but I hear they are sold on every street corner in Washington.

Gwendolen.

In Washington, should you be allowed out on a day pass, is filled with extraordinary women.

Cecily.

Do you mean like Ruth Bader Ginsburg and Nancy Pelosi?

Gwendolen.

There are other women in Washington. I am friends with many of the top Republican women.[With elaborate politeness.] Thank you. [Aside.] I feel like I am trapped in an episode of Real Housewives.

Cecily.

[Sweetly.] Really? Remind me who they are. Sugar? I don't take any myself. Sugar is just empty calories, not good for the body. I am on a low carb, low-sugar, high-protein, high-fiber, gluten-free, vegan, and fruitarian diet. But I am sure you eat lots of sugar.

Gwendolen.

[Superciliously.] No, thank you. [**Cecily** looks angrily at her, takes up the tongs, and puts four lumps of sugar into the cup.]

Cecily.

[Severely.] What do you eat?

Gwendolen.

[In a bored manner.] Nothing, that is how I lose weight. Besides, desserts are rarely seen at the best houses nowadays. I will have some celery sticks or tomato slices.

Cecily.

[Cuts a large slice of cake and puts it on the tray.] Hand that to Gwendolen.

[**Gayman** does so and goes out with footman. **Gwendolen** drinks the tea and makes a grimace. Puts down the cup at once, reaches out her hand to the celery, looks at it, and finds it is a cake that she squishes in her hands. She is horrified. Then she shoves both hands in her mouth, eating as if starving, in a sexual over-the-top Meg Ryan in Katz Deli way.]

Gwendolen.

[screames, now that she realizes she has eaten actual food, moves to flip table in RHONJ] You have filled my tea with lumps of sugar, and though I asked most distinctly for organic celery, you have given me cake. I am known for the gentleness of my disposition and the extraordinary sweetness of my nature, but I warn you, Cecily, you may go too far, I have swallowed that cake.

Cecily.
[Rising.] Just like Republican thinking, you can have your cake and eat it too.

Gwendolen.
Just like a Democrat thinking you can have someone else's cake.

Cecily.
For the record, I am not a Democrat, I am a progressive.

Gwendolen.
Well! That settles it. From the moment you opened your

mouth, I could tell no one was home. It seems as if I have wandered into some adult daycare center.

Cecily.

I imagine being a Republican in Washington; you would know all about that.

[Enter **Jane as Earnest**.]

Gwendolen.

[Catching sight of him.] Earnest! My own Earnest!

Jane as Earnest.

Gwendolen! Darling! [Offers to kiss her.]

Gwendolen.

[Draws back.] Affirmative Consent, darling. #NoBlurred-Lines. May I ask if you are engaged to be married to this young lady? [Points to **Cecily**.]

Jane as Earnest.

[Laughing.] To dear little Cecily! Of course not! What could have put such an idea into your pretty little head?

Gwendolen.

Thank you. You may! [Offers her cheek.]But no further till you put a ring on it.

Cecily.

[Very sweetly.] I knew there must be some misunderstanding, Gwennie dear. The woman whose arm is now round your waist is my guardian, Jane.

Gwendolen.

I beg your pardon.

Cecily.

This is Aunt Jane.

Gwendolen. Jane! Oh!

[Enter **Angie**.]

Cecily.

Here is Earnest.

Angie.

[Goes straight over to **Cecily** without noticing anyone else.]

My own love! [Offers to kiss her.]

Cecily.

[Drawing back.]

Hold up #MeToo May I ask you—are you engaged to be married to this young lady?

Angie.

[Looking round.] To what young lady? Good heavens! Gwendolen!

Cecily.

Yes! To this REPUBLICAN.

Angie as Earnest.

[Laughing.] Of course not! What could have put such an idea into your capable brain?

Cecily.

Thank you. [Presenting her cheek to be kissed.] You may. [**Angie** kisses her.]

Gwendolen.

I felt there was some slight error, Cecily. The person who is now embracing you is my cousin, Angie.

Cecily.

[Breaking away from **Angie**.] Angie! Oh!

[The two girls move towards each other and wrap their arms around their waists as if for protection.]

Cecily.

Please don't deadname them.

Angie.

I cannot deny it.

Cecily. Oh!

Gwendolen.

Is your name really Jane?

Jane as Earnest.

[Standing rather proudly.] I could deny it if I liked. I could deny anything if I liked. But my name certainly is Jane. It has been Jane for years.

Cecily.

[To **Gwendolen**.] A gross deception has been practiced on both of us.

Gwendolen.

Cecily!

Cecily.

Gwendolen! [Cecily and Gwendolen look longingly into each other's eyes as if to kiss]

Gwendolen.

[Slowly and seriously.] You will call me sister, will you not? [They embrace. **Jane** and **Angie** groan and walk up and down.]Not so close.I have one question. Why are you dressed like a lesbian soccer mom at Costco buying juice boxes? And Second, where is your brother Earnest? We are both engaged to be married to your brother Earnest, so it is important to us to know where your brother Earnest is at present.

Jane as Earnest.

I don't have a brother Earnest.

Cecily.

[Surprised.] No brother at all?

Jane as Earnest.

[Cheerily.] None!

Gwendolen.

[Severely.] Had you never a brother of any kind?

Jane as Earnest.

[Pleasantly.] Never. Not even of any kind.

Gwendolen.

I am afraid it is quite clear, Cecily, that neither of us is engaged to be married to anyone.

Cecily.

It is not a pleasant position for a young girl to suddenly find herself in. Is it?

Gwendolen.

Let's go inside. It seems we both have had too much time in the sun.

[They retire into the house with scornful looks.]

Jane as Earnest.

Bunburying, I suppose?

Angie.

This has been the most fun bun of my whole life.

Jane as Earnest.

You had no right to Bunbury here.

Angie.

I am a free-range Bunburyist.

Jane as Earnest.

You can't be serious.

Angie.

I don't mean to be serious.

Jane as Earnest.

The only satisfaction I get from this is that I get to be Earnest full-time.

Angie.

I don't know why you thought you had to hide Jane from me.

Jane as Earnest.

I guess I have been too, Earnest.

Angie.

As much as I welcome your transition, I don't see how Gwendolyn would ever accept someone who is transgender. She grew up steeped in the Christian Conservative tradition it will not come easy to her to accept a man in a woman's body. But why not tell Cecily? Surely she would have accepted you in whatever state you found yourself in.

Jane as Earnest.

I wasn't sure. Well, not completely. I wanted to see what it would be like before I came out. I just wanted what any man wants, a beautiful woman he can raise a family with, in that sense, we are very much alike.

Angie.

I just wanted to be engaged to Cecily, even though I just met her.

Jane as Earnest.

There is little chance of you sealing this deal.

Angie.

I doubt you are going to gain any ground with Gwendolyn.

Jane as Earnest.

You should stay out of my business.

Angie.

Love is not a business. It is very vulgar to talk about one's business. Only people like lobbyists do that, and then merely at dinner parties or whore houses.

Jane as Earnest.

How can you sit there when my whole life is coming apart?

Angie.

You will have your problems all stitched together soon.

Jane.

If Gwendolyn will be perfectly happy once I am done with

my transition. I am a man and she is a woman. What could be more natural? Nobody has to know.

Angie.

So the T is silent in LGB(whispers)T.

Jane

[Rising.] I am being serious. We will fly under the gaydar. No one will have to know.

Angie.

[Offering cake.] Don't you think it will come up eventually?

Jane.

Among our close friends, for sure, but I doubt Gwendolyn would want it out there. What we do behind closed doors is none of anyone's concern. Good heavens! Stop taking pictures of your food.

Angie.

It always surprises me how interested Republicans seem in what I do behind closed doors, especially when they are with me.

Jane.

I don't need to hear of your escapades in the closet.

Angie.

I will tell the tale one day, and who knows what might spill out.

Jane as Earnest.

Angie, I wish you would go.

Angie as Earnest.

You can't possibly ask me to go without having some dinner. It's absurd. I never go without my dinner. No one ever does, except vegetarians and intermittent fasters.

Jane as Earnest. I made arrangements this morning with Dr. Maker to turn my gherkin into a glorious cucumber. I have a perfect right to be whomever I like. For so much of my life, I have been in the wrong lane on a highway I didn't want to be on. I was driven to drive faster and faster when I only wanted to get in the wrong lane and into the right one. Now I am just looking for a top-notch stick shift to zoom the hell out of the rest of my life. It is different with you, your line of sight was always clear.

Angie as Earnest

I don't know if it was clear. Many things have changed in the community. Everyone expects you to be something else.

Jane as Earnest.

Slow down, Clark Kent. I am not trying to stop you from leaping over the capital in a single bound. I am transitioning, not you. My transition will be perfect; I will be able to write my entire name in the snow.

Angie.

Jane, you are at the macaroons again! I wish you wouldn't.

There are only two left. [Takes them.] I told you I was particularly fond of macaroons.

Jane.

But I hate cake.

Angie.

Why on earth then do you allow cake to be served up for your guests? What ideas you have of hospitality?

Jane.

Angie! I have already told you to go. I don't want you here. Why don't you go!

Angie.

I haven't quite finished my tea yet! And there is still one macaroon left. [**Jane** groans and sinks into a chair. **Angie** still continues eating.]

ACT DROP

Act Three

SCENE

Livingroom at the Manor House.

[**Gwendolen** and **Cecily** are at the window, looking out into the garden.]

Gwendolen.

The fact that they did not follow us at once into the house, as anyone else would have done, seems to me to show that they have some sense of shame left.

Cecily.

They have been eating macaroons. That looks like repentance.

Gwendolen.

[After a pause.] They don't seem to notice us at all. Couldn't you cough?

Cecily.

But I haven't got a cough.

Gwendolen.

They're looking right at us. How dare they!

Cecily. Wait, they are coming, act natural.

Gwendolen.

Not a word.

Cecily.

Certainly. It's the only thing to do now. [Enter **Jane** followed by **Angie**. They whistle a popular air from a Hamilton.]

Gwendolen.

This dignified silence seems to produce an unpleasant effect.

Cecily.

A most distasteful one.

Gwendolen.

But we will not be the first to speak.

Cecily.

Certainly not.

Gwendolen.

[to Jane] I have something very particular to ask you. Much depends on your reply.

Cecily.

Gwendolen, your common sense is invaluable. Angie, kindly

answer the following question. Why did you pretend to be my guardian's brother?

Angie.

To meet you.

Cecily.

[To **Gwendolen**.] works for me.

Gwendolen.

Everything works for you.

Cecily.

But that does not affect the wonderful beauty of the answer.

Gwendolen.

True. Why did you lie about having a brother? Was it in order that you might have an opportunity of coming up to town to see me as often as possible?

Jane.

Not exactly, I needed to live as Earnest. Meeting you as the real me was a blessing.

Gwendolen.

I am still not convinced. [Moving to **Cecily**.] You know all about this gender tender bender stuff, does that make sense to you?

Cecily.

I will validate that. It is not uncommon for people going

through transition to live as their true selves for a time out-side their immediate circle.

Gwendolen.

So does that mean I am a lesbian now?

Cecily.

Does it matter?

Gwendolen.

I imagine it will at some point.

Cecily.

Oh, Gwen, there is no gender anymore, there are no closets.

Gwendolen.

Does that mean we are all (swallows hard) "equal" now?

Cecily.

I wouldn't go that far. Just some are more equal than others.

Gwendolen.

Well, if I am one of the more equal ones, I accept.

Cecily.

Let's do it together.

Gwendolen. I am not that liberal.

Cecily.

Let's speak together.

Gwendolen.

An excellent idea!

Cecily.

Certainly. [**Gwendolen** beats time with an uplifted finger.]

Gwendolen and **Cecily** [

Speaking together. Gestures, hands cupped] We forgive you!

Jane and **Angie**

[Speaking together.] I love you.

Jane.

Now that that is all settled, I am headed to the Doctor Maker this afternoon.

Gwendolen.

[To **Jane.**] Are you going to do this for me?

Jane.

For you and myself. I have wanted a monument for as long as I can remember.

Cecily.

[To **Angie.**] Please never change.

Angie.

I won't.

Gwendolen.

All this talk about equality of the sexes when we were the same underneath all along

Jane.

We are for now. [Clasps hands with **Gwen**.]

Gwen.

I look forward to greeting the new arrival.

Gwendolen.

[To **Jane**.] My Husband!

Angie.

[To **Cecily**.] My Wife [They fall into each other's arms.]

[Enter **Gayman**. When he enters he coughs loudly, seeing the situation.]

Gayman. Ahem! Ahem! LadyBird Ball-Buster!

Jane. Uh oh.

[Enter **Lady Ball-Buster**. The couples separate in alarm. Exit **Gayman**.]

LadyBird Ball-Buster.

Gwendolen! What does this mean?

Gwendolen.

Merely that I am engaged to be married to .... I mean Earnest, mamma.

LadyBird Ball-Buster.

Come here. Sit down. Sit down immediately. Don't just stand there, sit down. [Turns to **Jane**.] Concetta told me of my daughter's sudden departure from the house-made, whose confidence I purchased by means of a threat to call ICE on her, I followed her at once by an Uber. Her unhappy father is, I am glad to say, under the impression that she is attending a more than usually lengthy lecture by Sean Hannity on how the media is the enemy of the people. I do not propose to undeceive him. Indeed I have never undeceived him on any question. I would consider it wrong. But of course, you will clearly understand that all communication between yourself and my daughter must cease immediately from this moment. Block him now.

Jane.

I am engaged to be married to Gwendolen, LadyBird Ball-Buster!

LadyBird Ball-Buster.

You are nothing of the kind, sir. And now, as regards Angie! … Angie!

Angie as Earnest.

Yes, Aunt LadyBird.

LadyBird Ball-Buster.

May I ask if it is in this house that your invalid friend Mr. Bunbury resides?

Angie.

[Stammering.] Oh! No! Bunbury doesn't live here. Bunbury is somewhere else at present. Bunbury is dead.

LadyBird Ball-Buster.

Dead! When did Mr. Bunbury die? His death must have been extremely sudden.

Angie.

[Airily.] Oh! I killed Bunbury this afternoon. I mean, poor Bunbury died this afternoon.

LadyBird Ball-Buster.

What did he die of?

Angie.

Bunbury? He was de-platformed for saying awful things on Twitter. It Killed him.

LadyBird Ball-Buster.

Parting is such a Tweet Sorrow. Was he a social provocateur like our sainted POTUS? May he rest forever in his social media death.

Angie.

Nothing so dramatic, Dear Aunt. Just a few ReTweets of some Russian accounts around the election.

LadyBird Ball-Buster.

Whatever could be wrong with that? Some of the best tweets I have seen about our Dear Leader and President for Life were in Russian. Now may I enquire who is the youngish lady to whom my niece, who, as I notice, is dressed like she is about to change her oil, is holding a little too closely. Please step back to make room for the holy spirit.

Jane.

That lady is Miss Cecily Cardew, my ward. [**LadyBird Ball-Buster** gives elevator eyes to **Cecily**.]

Angie.

I am engaged to be married to Cecily, Aunt LadyBird.

LadyBird Ball-Buster.

I beg your pardon.

Cecily.

Angie and I are engaged to be married, LadyBird.

LadyBird Ball-Buster.

That is Mrs. Ball-Buster to you. [With a shiver, crossing to the sofa and sitting down.] I do not know whether there is anything peculiarly exciting in the air of this particular part of Potomac, to make engagements a trending topic. I think some preliminary inquiry on my part would not be out of place. Earnest, is Miss Cardew connected with any of the larger railway stations in any of the major cities on the eastern seaboard? I merely desire information. Until yesterday I had no idea there were any families or persons whose origin was associated with the Terminus of the Acela line. [**Jane** looks perfectly furious, but restrains himself.]

Jane.

[In a clear, cold voice.] Cecily is the granddaughter of the late Mr. Thomas Cardew of Capitol Hill, Georgetown, and the Palisades.

Lady Ball-Buster.

Three addresses always inspire confidence, even in a politician. But what proof have I of their authenticity?

Jane.

It is on his Wikipedia page.

LadyBird Ball-Buster.

[Grimly.] I have known strange errors in that website.

Jane.

Cecily's family trust lawyers are Cox, Wiener, and Wang. They are very big in law.

LadyBird Ball-Buster.

Cox, Wiener, and Wang: an upstanding firm. Some of the biggest names in Washington are Cox. A firm of the very highest position in their profession. Indeed I am told Mr. Wiener can be seen at the Palm.

Jane.

[Very irritably.] I think you will find a Cox, Wiener, or Wang at the center of nearly every scandal in Washington.

LadyBird Ball-Buster.

I try to avoid such things. [Rises, looks at her watch.]

Gwendolen! We must leave now. We have not a moment to lose. As a matter of form, Earnest, I had better ask you if Cecily has a few shekels in the bank.

Jane.

Oh! About a 1.7 billion in Amazon stock.

LadyBird Ball-Buster.

[Sitting down again.] A moment, Ms. Worthing. One point seven billion! And in Amazon stock! Now that I look at her, Miss Cardew seems to me a most attractive young lady. Few girls of the present day have any really solid qualities, any of the qualities that last and pay dividends with time. I regret to say we live in an age of selfies and cynicism. [To **Cecily.**] Come over here, dear. [**Cecily** goes across.] Pretty child! Your dress is pretty basic, and your hair seems almost as All mighty lord Jesus Christ might have left it. But we can soon alter all that. A thoroughly experienced homosexual hairdresser produces a marvelous result in a brief time. I had a wonderful hairdresser, but he beat himself up on the way home from sweaty sodomite liaison. It is a shame he did wonders with my coiff. I remember recommending him to young Ivanka Trump, and after three months, her father did not know her.

Jane.

That must have been a great relief to her.

LadyBird Ball-Buster.

[Glares at **Jane** for a few moments. Then bends, with a

practiced smile, to **Cecily**.] Kindly turn round, sweet child. [**Cecily** turns completely round.] No, the side view is what I want. [**Cecily** presents her profile.] Yes, quite as I expected. There are distinct social possibilities in your profile. Your nose is in the correct proportions. Any large, and we would be questioning your religion. We might have to shave that nose down slightly to remove any ambiguity. There is a doctor who can wasp you up. Perhaps breast implants. They are worn very high this season. Yours could use a pep talk; they are slightly depressed……Angie!

Angie.

Yes, Aunt LadyBird?

LadyBird Ball-Buster.

There are distinct possibilities in Miss Cardew's profile.

Angie.

Cecily is the sweetest, dearest, prettiest girl on Instagram. And I don't care a bitcoin about social possibilities. [LadyBird gasps]

LadyBird Ball-Buster.

Never speak disrespectfully of Insta, Angie. Only people who can't get followers do that. [To **Cecily**.] Dear child, of course you know that Angie has nothing but his debts. When I married Mr. Ballbuster I had no money, just a little talent. But I never dreamed for a moment of allowing that to stand in my way. Well, I suppose I must give my consent.

Angie.

Thank you, Aunt LadyBird.

LadyBird Ball-Buster.

Cecily, you may kiss me!

Cecily.

[Kisses her.] Thank you, LadyBird Ball-Buster.

LadyBird Ball-Buster.

You may also address me as Aunt LadyBird for the future.

Cecily.

Thank you, Aunt LadyBird.

LadyBird Ball-Buster.

[Cecily and Angie are all over each other] The marriage, I think, had better take place quite soon.

Jane.

Thank you, Aunt LadyBird, right after I get a long-awaited package.

Gwendolyn.

Thank you, Mother.

LadyBird Ball-Buster.

To speak frankly, I do not favor long engagements; it gives you too much time to change your mind.

Jane.

I beg your pardon for interrupting you, LadyBird Ball-Buster, but this engagement is out of the question. I am Cecily's guardian, and she cannot marry without my consent until she comes of age. That consent I absolutely decline to give.

LadyBird Ball-Buster.

On what grounds, may I ask? Angie is available, and she already has the Uhaul.

Jane.

It pains me very much to speak frankly to you, Mrs. Ballbuster, about your niece, but she has been deceiving you! [**Angie** and **Cecily** look at her in indignant amazement.]

LadyBird Ball-Buster.

Untruthful! My niece Angie? Impossible! She is a Republican. [Angie mouths no and waves hands behind LadyBird's back] We don't deceive unless it is to hide something.

Jane.

I fear there can be no possible doubt about the matter. This afternoon during my temporary absence in DC on an important question of romance, she obtained admission to my house by means of the false pretense of being my brother. Under an assumed name she drank, I've just been informed by my butler, an entire pint bottle of my Jack Daniels Black; I was specially reserving for myself. Continuing her disgraceful deception, she succeeded in wooing Cecily during the afternoon. And what makes her conduct all the more heartless is, that she was perfectly well aware from the first that I have no brother, that I never had a brother, and that I don't intend to have a brother, not even of any kind. I distinctly told her so myself yesterday afternoon.

LadyBird Ball-Buster.

Ahem! Earnest, after careful consideration, I have decided entirely to overlook my nieces-nephews mild deceptions. We live in a post-truth world now, and one must adjust to the reality of not having facts.

Jane.

That is very generous of you, LadyBird Ball-Buster. My own decision, however, is unalterable. I decline to give my consent.

LadyBird Ball-Buster.

[To **Cecily**.] Come here, sweet child. [**Cecily** goes over.] How old are you, dear?

Cecily.

I am almost eighteen, but I always admit to twenty-one when I go to bars.

LadyBird Ball-Buster.

You are perfectly right in making some slight alterations. Indeed, no woman should ever be quite accurate about her age. It looks so calculating . . . [In a meditative manner.] Eighteen, but admitting to twenty-one. Well, it will not be very long before you are of age and free from the bounds of your age or we could go to another state.

Jane.

Pray, excuse me, Lady Ballbuster, for interrupting you again, but it is only fair to tell you that according to the terms of her grandfather's will, Cecily does not come to get the money until she is thirty-five.

LadyBird Ball-Buster.

Thirty-five? Angie might be ready for a second wife by then. Though thirty-five is a very attractive age. DC society is full of women who have remained thirty-five for years of their own free choice. Speaker Pelosi has refused to age at all. To my own knowledge, she has been thirty-five ever since she arrived at the age of forty, which was many years ago now. I see no reason why our dear Cecily's fortune should not be more attractive in a few years. There will be a large accumulation of property.

Cecily.

Angie, could you wait for me till I was thirty-five?

Angie.

I would have you know and then have the money too, it is ideal.

Cecily.

I am not punctual myself, I know, but I do like punctuality in others, and waiting, even to be married, is quite out of the question.

Angie.

Then what is to be done, Cecily?

Cecily.

I don't know, Angie.

LadyBird Ball-Buster.

My dear Earnest, Cecily states positively that they will marry anyway without (coughs).... the money. There is little more to be done.

Jane.

If Mrs. Ball-Buster, you consent to my marriage with Gwendolen, I will most gladly allow the funds to be available on the wedding day.

LadyBird Ball-Buster.

[Rising and drawing herself up.] You must be aware that what you propose is out of the question.

Jane.

Think of all that money just sitting there.

LadyBird Ball-Buster.

Still, it is the principle of the thing. Love is fleeting, but money is forever. [Pulls out her watch.] Come, dear, [**Gwendolen** rises] we have already missed five if not six, ubers. To miss any more might expose us to a bad rating. It is hard to get a pickup for anything less than five stars. I miss the days when you could pay off the driver when something went amiss.

[Enter **Dr. Maker.**]

Maker.

Everything is quite ready for the new arrivals.

LadyBird Ball-Buster.

New arrivals? Are you both pregnant? That does not make sense. I have someone who can take care of that. I am pro-life to the core unless it is my daughter or GOP fundraiser, my husband's "friends," and then it is acceptable.

Maker.

[Looking rather puzzled and pointing to **Jane** and **Angie.**] Earnest has expressed a desire for gender reassignment.

LadyBird Ball-Buster.

The idea is grotesque and irreligious! What is wrong with the gender that you already have? I will not allow you to become a woman. You are a man and will stay a man. I was just getting used to the gay thing. Women are naturally superior in every way except in their paychecks, advancement opportunities, presidential candidacy, and control of their reproductive life. Gaylord Ballbuster would be highly displeased if he learned that that was the way in which you wasted your time and money.

Maker.

No surgery then?

Jane.

Yes, it will, Dr. Maker.

Maker.

This is a very serious decision, one that is not taken lightly. Indeed, I have just been informed by my receptionist that for the last hour and a half, Miss Presbyopia has been waiting for me to have an opening.

LadyBird Ball-Buster.

[Starting.] Miss Presbyopia! Did I hear you mention Miss Presbyopia?

Maker.

Yes, LadyBird Ball-Buster. I am on my way to join her.

LadyBird Ball-Buster.

Pray, allow me to detain you for a moment. This matter may prove to be one of vital importance to Mr. Ball-Buster and me. Is this Miss Presbyopia, a female of marginal looks, remotely connected with education?

Maker.

[Somewhat indignantly.] She is the most cultivated of ladies and the very picture of respectability.

LadyBird Ball-Buster.

It is the same person. May I ask what position she hold
for you?

Maker.

[Severely.] Well, not yet. We are friends with benefits yet
to be determined.

Jane.

[Interposing.] Miss Presbyopia has been Cecil's homeschool
teacher for the last three years.

LadyBird Ball-Buster.

It is good that you kept Cecilhy out of the public education
system; some flowers bloom best in their own garden. You
wouldn't want the wrong type of African bee around this
lily-white flower.

[Enter **Miss Presbyopia** hurriedly.]

Miss Presbyopia.

I was told you expected me in your office, dear Dick. I
have been waiting for you for an hour. [Catches sight of
LadyBird Ballbuster, who has fixed her with a stony glare.
Miss Presbyopia grows pale and fake swoons. She looks
anxiously round as if desirous to escape.]

LadyBird Ball-Buster.

[In a severe, judicial voice.] Presbyopia! [**Miss Presbyopia**
bows her head in shame.] Come here, Presbyopia! [**Miss
Presbyopia** approaches in a humble manner.] Presbyopia!

Where is that baby? [General consternation. The **Doctor** starts back in horror. **Angie** and **Jane** pretend to be anxious to shield **Cecily** and **Gwendolen** from hearing the details of a terrible public scandal.] Twenty-eight years ago, Presbyopia, you left Gaylord Ballbuster's house, Number 1601, Pennsylvania Ave, in charge of a children's stroller that contained a baby of the female sex. You never returned. A few weeks later, through the elaborate investigations of the DC police, the stroller was discovered at midnight, standing by itself in a remote corner of Union Station. It contained the screenplay of a three-part Dom-Com bondage movie about a tech start-up sociopath who falls in love with a virgin whom he makes his sex slave. 49 Shades of Red [**Miss Presbyopia** starts in involuntary indignation.] But the baby was not there! [Everyone looks at **Miss Presbyopia**.] Presbyopia! Where is that baby? [A pause.]

Miss Presbyopia.

Lady Ballbuster, I admit with shame that I do not know. I only wish I did. The plain facts of the case are these. On the morning of the day you mentioned, a day that is forever branded on my memory, I prepared, as usual, to take the baby out in its stroller. I also had with me a somewhat old, but capacious coach bag in which I had intended to place the screenplay I had written during my few unoccupied hours. In a moment of mental abstraction, for which I never can forgive myself, I deposited the manuscript in the carriage and placed the baby in the handbag.

Jane.

[Who has been listening attentively.] But where did you deposit the coach bag?

Miss Presbyopia.

Do not ask me.

Jane.

Miss Presbyopia, this is a matter of no small importance to me. I insist on knowing where you deposited that infant's coach bag.

Miss Presbyopia.

I left it in the Starbucks at Union Station.

Jane.

Which Starbucks?

Miss Presbyopia.

[Quite crushed.] By the Biden Line to Delaware. [Sinks into a chair.]

Jane.

I must go to my room for a moment. Gwendolen, wait here for me.

Gwendolen.

If you are not too long, I will wait for you all my life. [Exit **Jane** in great excitement.]

Maker.

What do you think this means, LadyBird?

LadyBird Ball-Buster.

I dare not even suspect Dr. Maker. I need hardly tell you that in families of high positions, strange coincidences are not supposed to occur. But it seems we have misplaced something.

[Noises heard overhead as if someone was throwing trunks about. Everyone looks up.]

Cecily.

Earnest seems strangely agitated.

Maker.

A little testosterone will clear up that condition. Earnest will be thrilled to be unburdened by emotions.

LadyBird Ball-Buster.

This noise is extremely unpleasant. It sounds as if he was arguing. I dislike arguments of any kind. They are always vulgar and often convincing.

Maker.

[Looking up.] It has stopped now. [The noise is redoubled.]

LadyBird Ball-Buster.

I wish he would arrive at some conclusion.

Gwendolen.

This suspense is terrible. I hope it will last. [Enter **Jane** with a coach of black leather in his hand.]

Jane.

[Rushing over to **Miss Presbyopia**.] Is this the coach bag, Miss Presbyopia? Examine it carefully before you speak. The happiness of more than one life depends on your answer.

Miss Presbyopia.

[Calmly.] It seems to be mine. Yes, here is the injury it received through upsetting a Crosstown circulator Street omnibus in younger and happier days. Here is the stain on the lining caused by a small flask beverage explosion. And here, on the lock, are my initials. I had forgotten that, in an extravagant mood, I had had them placed there. The bag is undoubtedly mine. I am delighted to have it so unexpectedly restored to me. It has been a great inconvenience being without it all these years.

Jane.

[In a pathetic voice.] Miss Presbyopia, more is restored to you than this coach bag. I was the baby you placed in it.

Miss Presbyopia.

[Amazed.] You?

Jane.

[Embracing her.] Yes . . . mother!

Miss Presbyopia.

[Recoiling in indignant astonishment.] I am unmarried!

Jane.

Who of us has not risked seeing the stork before the preacher? [Tries to embrace her again.]

Miss Presbyopia.

[Still more indignant.] Not me. [Pointing to **LadyBird Ball-Buster.**] There is a lady who can tell you who you really are.

Jane.

[After a pause.] LadyBird Ballbuster, I hate to seem inquisitive, but would you kindly inform me who I am?

LadyBird Ball-Buster.

You are the daughter of my sister and, consequently, Angie's elder sister.

Jane.

Angie's elder brother, not sister, brother!

LadyBird Ball-Buster.

I just found my niece and lost her to my nephew. I am still not quite recovered from the unfortunate aspects of allowing homo-sexuals rights. You cannot make me recognize any more of your alphabet soup world, LQBVSTLG. I don't care. The transgender thing is just a step too far for me. You will kindly stop telling me what pronouns to use and what to call people. It is just too much.

Jane.

Aunt LadyBird, I have spent my entire life being told who I am and can love. Maybe **I am** just a little tired of being told what to do too. If you are said to use a pronoun, you don't agree with for a few seconds; suddenly, you think you are oppressed. You don't know what oppression is until you walk out of a club, praying to G-d above that you make it home without being killed.

LadyBird Ball-Buster.

Don't be so dramatic. All I ever hear is how repressed you are, in my opinion. I say good. Be repressed. It is what makes society run. Stay gay; we have a few at my church even. But don't get this mutilation done. Leave your body just as the good lord intended it.

Gwendolyn.

Oh, mamma, you have spent more money on plastic surgery, fillers, botox, and dermabrasions than on charity in the last three years. You are hardly one to talk about keeping your body as G-d made it.

LadyBird.

That is hardly the same thing. I am just making a few minor repairs. Inside I still feel like a young woman, and outside when I look in the mirror, I see someone else staring back at me, someone I am not sure I recognize.

Jane.

That **is** how I feel. I look in the mirror and see the wrong person looking back at me. It is a person that I don't recognize. But if I turn a certain way or cock my head sideways, I can see the faintest glimpse of who I am. Like you, I want the outside to match the inside.

Lady Bird. Maybe I do understand just a little. So this is my nephew.

Angie.

And this is my brother. [Seizes hold of **Jane.**] Dr. Maker, my brother. Miss Presbyopia, my brother. Gwendolen, my brother. Earnest, you have been mean, borrowed my clothes, we have fought in the streets, been drunk together, had that night at the Watergate.. never mind. You have been my brother the whole time.

Angie.

Brother

[Shakes hands.]

Gwendolen.

[To **Jane.**] My love! But what do I call you? Jane or Earnest

Jane.

Good heavens! Gwen, I thought you understood. My name is Earnest.

Gwendolen.

This is so confusing, who am I really in love with? Am I a lesbian?

LadyBird Ball-Buster.

For heaven's sake. Now Gwen is gay? What is in the water out here?

Cecily.

Gwen, you can be whoever you want to be. Call yourself whatever you want. We accept you just as you are. It is what it means to be a progressive unless you use the wrong pronoun or support Israel.

LadyBird Ball-Buster.

Our dear leader is very fond of the Hebrews, up to a point.

Jane.

But LadyBird, what was my birth name?

LadyBird Ball-Buster.

I can't remember. It has been some time.

Jane.

[Irritably.] You can remember.

LadyBird Ball-Buster.

[Meditatively.] I cannot, at the present moment, recall what the Judge's first name was. But I have no doubt he had one. But everyone just called him Judge. Not sure why he never practiced law.

Jane.

Angie! Can't you remember what our dad's name was

Angie.

I can't remember more than Dada; he passed before I was one.

Jane.

Was he a man of some means, was he not, Aunt LadyBird?

LadyBird Ball-Buster.

The Judge was a man of many opinions, all liberal drivel about feeding the poor and providing free healthcare and job training.

Jane.

I bet he has a Wikipedia page if nothing else but to spite Aunt LadyBird. Let me see, Earnest John. [Puts phone down.] I told you, Gwendolen, my name was Earnest, didn't I? After Dr. Maker makes a big change, I will always be Earnest.

LadyBird Ball-Buster.

Yes, I remember now that the Judge was called Earnest, I never liked people being Earnest. That is why I only watch Fox News…..or RT.

Gwendolen.

Earnest! I knew all along that was your true name.

Jane.

Gwennie, is is an awful thing to know that all along you have been telling nearly the truth your whole life.

Gwendolen.

I am sure that will change over time.

Jane.

My dear!

Maker.

[To **Miss Presbyopia**.] Labia! [Embraces her]

Miss Presbyopia.

[Enthusiastically.] Dick! At last!

Angie.

Cecily! [Embraces her.] At last!

Jane.

Gwendolen! [Embraces her.] At last!

LadyBird Ball-Buster.

Earnest, you are displaying all the signs of being a true Republican.

Jane.

On the contrary, Aunt BallBuster, I've now realized for the first time in my life the Importance of Being Earnest.

About the Author

As a passionate writer and theater enthusiast based in Washington, DC, A.J. Campbell has always been drawn to Oscar Wilde's works' intricate wit and timeless themes. With a deep appreciation for the arts and a desire to innovate within the field, A.J. founded The Quarantine Players, a virtual theater company, as a creative response to the unprecedented times of global lockdowns. This adaptation of 'The Importance of Being Earnest' is a tribute to Wilde's genius and a testament to A.J.'s dedication to keeping the spirit of theater alive in challenging times. By reimagining this classic through a contemporary lens, A.J. seeks to engage audiences in a dialogue that bridges the past and the present, showcasing the enduring relevance of Wilde's sharp social commentary.